OUT *of the* DROWNING DEEP

Also by A. C. Wise and available from Titan Books

Wendy, Darling
Hooked

OUT
of the
DROWNING
DEEP

A. C.
WISE

TITAN BOOKS

Out of the Drowning Deep
Print edition ISBN: 9781803369822
E-book edition ISBN: 9781803369839

Published by Titan Books
A division of Titan Publishing Group Ltd
144 Southwark Street, London SE1 0UP
www.titanbooks.com

First edition: September 2024
10 9 8 7 6 5 4 3 2 1

A CIP catalogue record for this title is available from
the British Library.

Printed and bound by CPI Group (UK) Ltd, Croydon,
CR0 4YY.

For Scott Andrews. This book is inadvertently his fault.

1

The sky above the Bastion deepened into the green of an old bruise. One moon slashed a sickle-cut, another waxed full, the third crept up from the horizon, a chain of stars looping all three. Atop the most crumbling and unloved tower of the once-glorious Mecca, now broken open to the sky, Scribe IV tilted his head back and tried to guess where Heaven's Ark Station stood in its orbit at that moment.

It would be easy to find out, satellite relays pinpointing the station with near-perfect accuracy. But when so many great questions had been answered – the nature of gods and angels, the shape of the universe – Scribe IV chose to find mystery wherever he could. However small. He craved wonder, and the possibility that at any moment he might experience uncertainty, be surprised.

It was like the aging shield that protected the open tower from the worst of the elements. It shuddered occasionally, making the sky beyond it seem to shimmer, but he chose to see beauty, rather than flawed technology that needed to be replaced. And in the same way, it was vastly preferable to guess every now and then, rather than having every stray pondering answered in nanoseconds with the mere flick of his fingers.

"Sir?" A voice in the doorway; Scribe IV turned to the Page shifting from foot to foot on the threshold. "The Chatelaine reports all preparations are complete and ready for your final inspection, though she still doesn't seem happy about it, sir."

Dominic paused, waiting to see if Scribe IV would take the bait. He decided to indulge the boy. "Oh? Why do you say that?"

"I don't think she approves of the Pope, sir," Dominic said. "And I don't think she's happy about the conclave."

"That may be," Scribe IV said, "but even if so, that is none of our business, is it?"

The gentle reprimand appeared to leave Dominic a little crestfallen. He'd clearly been prepared to gossip, but Scribe IV always endeavored to model good manners for the boy when he could. Whether the Chatelaine did or did not like the Pope – much like Scribe IV's own opinions on the Chatelaine – was not an appropriate topic for discussion.

"Please proceed with your report," Scribe IV prompted.

Dominic brightened. He took pride in his duties, which Scribe IV appreciated.

"His Holiness is settled in. The Bastion is ready to welcome the rest of the conclave."

"Thank you, Dominic," Scribe IV said. "You've done very well."

He inclined his head to the boy. As the youngest member of the Bastion's sparse staff, Scribe IV too often saw Dominic treated with dismissive impatience, as if his age made him a burden, always underfoot. He did whatever he could to counterbalance that – extending patience, kindness, and the same level of courtesy he accorded to the rest of the staff, whether or not they deserved it.

"And the tea service was brought to His Holiness's room exactly an hour after his supper, as he requested?" Scribe IV asked.

"Yes, sir." Scribe IV saw the boy suppress an urge to fidget. "I heard Johanna, I mean the Chatelaine, say she wanted to put the tray together herself while I was in the kitchen. Seb was just about to give me an extra shortbread but she yelled at me for being in the way even though I was trying to help."

Dominic looked regretful over the lost shortbread, and resentful over his treatment. Scribe IV couldn't blame the boy. There were times he wished he'd been programmed for less politeness, so he could tell the Chatelaine exactly what he thought of her and the way she treated those she saw as her inferiors.

The best he could do was take an occasional, bitter pleasure in sending her and the other members of staff he considered rude on errands through the network of tunnels winding under the Bastion. While he never sent them anywhere truly dangerous, into the collapsed lower sections for instance, the storage areas were bad enough. Even those who didn't believe the tunnels were god-haunted had to contend with the dark and the damp. Since so many members of the human staff were determined to dislike him, Scribe IV felt he might as well give them a reason. The tunnels were just one of their battlegrounds.

Dominic, on the other hand, was always thrilled to run errands in the tunnels. They were the perfect place for a boy his age to burn off energy, not to mention the most exciting thing about the Bastion, as far as the Page was concerned.

Even though they complained, Scribe IV knew both the Chatelaine and the Head Butler often left small shrines and prayers down in the dark. He found keys left behind like offerings, as if the Chatelaine's god would hear her more clearly in a place that had once been so holy, that echoed with so much faith.

"Will there be anything else, sir?" Dominic asked.

Naked hope, barely disguised, turned the boy into a coiled spring. Since Johanna had shooed him away from making himself useful in the kitchen earlier, Scribe IV saw no reason not to let Dominic entertain himself or watch the rest of the preparations as he chose. While he'd never been young, Scribe IV had been new once and could recall the thrill that came with the prospect of a day unlike any other, a break from routine. The Bastion – part fortress, part library, part cathedral – was an all-but-forgotten waystation these days, a relic like Scribe IV himself. A pilgrim might spend the night, or a scholar visit to consult an obscure tome in person, but otherwise there was nothing here but the watchful moons, the endless boom of the tide, and the slow, inevitable march of entropy.

"Thank you, Dominic. Nothing further. You are free for the rest of the day," Scribe IV said.

Scribe IV's features had not been designed to convey warmth or fondness. His expression was now as it had been nearly a century ago, hammered into copper as serene, neutral and unchanging. The best he could do was incline his head again.

"Thank you, sir!"

Like a loosed arrow, the boy shot from the doorway, turning long enough to flash him a quicksilver grin before clattering down the stairs just ahead of gravity and dashing off through the Bastion's maze of passages. Off to snatch gossip like a bird carried crumb – not to mention snatching a few actual crumbs as well, including the shortbread he'd been chased away from earlier. Seb would have kept it aside for him. The Cook had taken a shine to Dominic, even teaching him a few basic kitchen skills when he could convince the boy to stay still long enough.

Scribe IV listened to Dominic's footsteps until he could no longer hear them. Had he ever lived that fast and bright? Unlikely, but once upon a time he'd wished to, longing for a blood-beating heart and breath in place of gears, to choose his destiny instead of being purpose-built. It was there in his name: Scribe IV – amanuensis, designed to copy holy books, to record prayers, and nothing more.

In his own way, he was as trapped as the Bastion's human staff, though very few of them saw it that way. Scribe IV found peace and comfort in the Bastion, yet he might have sympathized with the staff, living their lives in a dying, crumbling ruin. Most had nowhere else they could go.

But so many of them took their bitterness, their disappointed faith, and turned it outward – resenting Scribe IV, seeing him as an object of disgust, or pity. A useless creation whose very existence mocked the gods.

As if he'd asked to be placed above them. Guardianship of the Bastion had fallen to him based merely on tenure. At the time he'd assumed oversight, the Bastion had been in the midst of its last great exodus; there'd been no one else to take the job. It wasn't even an enviable position. The Bastion had been in decline for years; soon enough, Scribe IV would be guardian of nothing at all.

Which, on the surface, made it strange that His Holiness had chosen the Bastion, of all forsaken places, for a conclave of as many representatives of the fractured multitude of religions as he could convince to join him.

Scribe IV understood the symbolism. The Pope had chosen the Bastion for its history as much as its seclusion. It was on this spot, on the perilous cliffs above the sea, that the gods had first made themselves known. Definitive proof of angels and demons, of unnamed and eldritch horrors, of all the still-worshipped gods of Earth and all the forgotten ones – the animal-headed, the many-armed, the ineffable beings of light. They had all come together here for one brief, terrible, shining moment.

It should have ushered in a new age of peace – and it had briefly, before immediately unraveling again, humans being what they were. That was what the Pope sought again now. His conclave would take place in the Bastion's Great Dining Hall, whose massive bronze doors and many stained-glass windows depicted that divine first meeting of the gods. Under all those watchful glass and bronze eyes, the Pope intended to propose the abolishment of all established religions.

He seemed to believe that the gathered clerics and priests, nuns and monks, mullahs and rabbis, would unanimously agree with him. That they would abdicate their roles, step aside and put religion directly back into the hands of the people. All churches, temples, synagogues and houses of worship would be left to rot. All holy offices, including the Pope's own, would be dissolved.

It was an absurd idea. Scribe IV had experienced enough trouble simply getting the invited guests to agree on the inconsequential choice of a menu for the welcome dinner. Still, he admired the Pope's sheer gall, his faith in the goodness of humanity, even if he fully expected the assembled priests, acolytes, vestal virgins and prophets to fall upon him for his words and tear him apart.

It wasn't his job to question the Pope's wisdom. His only job was to ensure the proceedings went as smoothly as possible – even if the success of the Pope's plan, against all odds, would likely mean the end of the Bastion.

Scribe IV tried not to dwell on what would happen to those under his care then. As much as they resented him, he didn't want to see the staff turned out into the universe's uncaring cold. Many of them had never known any other life than this place, had been abandoned here as children – like Agnetta, like the former Head Chambermaid Justine, like Dominic. What else was there for them? Heaven's Ark, like most stations, was highly selective about bringing new workers on board. The mining colonies around Ganymede would take anyone, as would the Junker ships salvaging scrap on an endless loop between the stars, but those were as good as a death sentence. At least in the Bastion, the staff were fed and clothed. If they were unhappy here, perhaps they had not closely considered their alternatives.

For his part, Scribe IV had found something like peace in his quiet and strange existence. He was obsolete, like the Bastion. Time had moved past him; he and this place were perfectly suited to each other. Under the green sky, above the booming surf, he could forget about the speed of technology, the speed of human life, and cling to the illusion that mysteries still existed. Most days, he could convince himself that he was content, that this crumbling existence was enough.

Precisely nine minutes and thirty-seven seconds after Scribe IV dismissed Dominic, a scream echoed through the Bastion.

Scribe IV levered himself up from his desk, away from the quills and ink pots, tools of his trade. One of his quirks – digital paper with its re-usable smart ink had replaced the need for the originals, but he preferred the old ways. He felt the weight of age in his finely wrought bones, in the gears and the wires of him, as he descended from his tower to see about the noise.

He nearly collided with the Chatelaine at the foot of the stairs.

"What happened?" he asked.

The Chatelaine shook her head, eyes wide, lips pressed into a thin line. Her fingers knotted in a complex pattern that drained the blood from them – a nervous gesture, or an arcane prayer. Keys chimed around her waist, every shape, every size, sewn all along her sleeves and stitched to every available scrap of her clothing.

"Show me," Scribe IV said.

The Chatelaine ducked her head, not out of respect, but as if trying to escape being seen by something terrible. Had she been coming to find him, or had she been running away?

She led him back the way she'd come. Scribe IV's steps – his feet molded in the approximation of human bones, but much less flexible – rang on the stone.

The Chatelaine stopped, gesturing to the Head Chambermaid, who sat on a narrow wooden chair someone had dragged into the hallway. The Head Butler stood beside her, one hand on the distraught woman's shoulder, the barest tips of his fingers resting against the fabric of her uniform, as if he feared her distress might be contagious.

Johanna, the Chatelaine; Anna-Maria, the Head Chambermaid; and Marius, the Head Butler. Each had been at the Bastion for over fifteen years now, and all reported directly to Scribe IV. Only Anna-Maria had any staff left under her – Agnetta, the Chambermaid. Not that it stopped Johanna from issuing orders to everyone around her, as if the Bastion were hers to control.

Scribe IV wondered at the three of them, clustered together in this hallway. It made him uneasy. He assumed Anna-Maria had been the one to scream. Perhaps the other two had simply followed the sound, as he had.

"What happened?" Scribe IV repeated his question, crouching to bring his face level with Anna-Maria.

He recognized the room she sat outside. He wished he did not.

Anna-Maria didn't look up. He set his fingers under her chin as gently as he could, giving her no choice but to look at him.

Her eyes widened. She had never liked him, found his presence, his guardianship of this place, profane.

"I thought the boy had stolen something, the way he ran," Anna-Maria said.

The boy – she meant Dominic.

"I only went inside to see what he might've nicked. I thought the room must be empty and that's why he was there – but then I saw the body."

Unease became dread, ticking down each brass knob of Scribe IV's spine.

"Nothing's been touched," Johanna interjected.

She took up a position at Anna-Maria's other shoulder. There was something possessive and defensive in the gesture, meant to convey that the three of them were a united front against him.

Johanna held Scribe IV's gaze, chin lifted. Metal shivered on metal, keys ringing along her sleeve. She made no offer to unlock the door for him, no move to hand over a key. Humans and their little games of power.

Scribe IV knew for a fact there weren't enough doors in the Bastion for that many keys. The Chatelaine had made her station her own religion.

During the age of splintering, some dug harder into established religions, renewing their faith and devotion to their old gods. Others sought to raise up new gods, thinking if they could attach themselves even to something as simple as a key and imbue it with enough belief, that key would eventually become a god, and they would be favored in the new god's eyes.

Scribe IV had seen the tail-end of that age. It wasn't only inanimate objects that were raised, but people too. He'd seen mortal flesh and carven masks made divine, wicked men and empty vessels of blown glass elevated, seemingly without rhyme or reason. He'd seen the disastrous and tragic results of forced divinity. And he'd seen the glory when true divinity took hold.

Scribe IV wondered if the Chatelaine's keys had ever answered her prayers; whether she, in fact, felt divine.

He straightened, joints slow to respond. "What happened to the boy?" he asked.

Johanna shook her head, lips pressed thin again. Anna-Maria also remained silent. Either she didn't know, or didn't believe he deserved an answer. Scribe IV rarely regretted his lack of breath, but the urge to sigh was almost overwhelming.

"The key, please."

The Chatelaine hesitated a moment, then handed it over, managing to convey resentment with the gesture.

Scribe IV unlocked the door, slipping the key into the pocket of his own robe rather than returning it – human pettiness had rubbed off on him – and stepped across the threshold. He closed the door behind him before any of the others could follow.

A body lay sprawled on the floor on the far side of the neatly made bed. The tea service still sat on the table against the wall, used, the cup replaced neatly on the tray. Agnetta, the Chambermaid, had not yet come to take it away.

Scribe IV crouched next to the body. A hooded robe covered the corpse's face, made from simple, heavy wool of a brown deep enough to be almost black, belted with a rope. No blood pooled on the floor, the cause of death not immediately obvious.

Poison. Suffocation. Blunt force trauma, delivered in such a skillful way that it left no mark, all damage internal. A heart attack. Scribe IV catalogued the ways a human body might fail or be forced into failure. He was stalling. He knew whose room this was, whose body this must be, and he did not want it to be true. Until he drew the hood back, looked at the corpse's face, there was still a sliver of a chance that everything hadn't gone horribly wrong, that he didn't have a disaster on his hands.

A curl of paper caught his eye, tucked into the corpse's hand. He tugged it free – the death was recent enough that the fingers were not yet stiff, and it came away easily. Blank. He felt the urge to sigh again. Had he really expected it to be so easy, that the killer would leave a signed confession behind?

The paper reminded him of nothing so much as the scrolls he himself used to record prayers. It might be here by accident and mean nothing at all. Or it might mean everything. He tucked it away between the bones of his arm, copper-sheened, exposed as his maker had designed them, then readjusted his sleeve to cover it.

He could no longer avoid the body itself.

He moved the fabric hood as gently as possible. A deeply profane litany shot across his synapses, but at least he refrained from expressing it aloud.

Fuckthemostholygodsandalltheirangels.

The slim chance vanished. The disaster became real. The dead body was none other than His Holiness, the Pope.

As if Scribe IV's confirmation were a swift flying from the ruined towers to spread the news, change fell over the Bastion. The air pressure and temperature dropped. The shades of the sky deepened from the dark purple of old blood to a sullen gray. Behind the piling clouds, the distant stars shivered.

The first bell tolled.

It was a sound felt as much as heard, resonating in Scribe IV's bones.

He'd hoped never to hear that bell again. How by all that was holy and awful did they know, when he himself had only just learned? Had their cursed god spoken to them in dreams, prophesied the precise day and hour of this pope's demise, so that they'd be ready to spring into action when the time came?

A second toll followed the first, then a third, going on and on. A clarion call to take heed; the Sisters of the Drowned Deep were coming.

That alone told Scribe IV that the Pope's death had not been accidental or natural. He'd craved mystery in his life; now he had a murder on his hands.

Scribe IV rose from his crouch beside the dead Pope. Perhaps it was sacrilege, but he left the body where it was, relocking the door behind him. He made a point of letting Johanna see him holding onto the key.

"No one is to enter this room except by my express permission," Scribe IV said. He waited for one of the three to challenge him, but none of them did. "That is all. You're dismissed."

They hesitated; again, Scribe IV expected defiance, but Marius helped Anna-Maria to stand, and he and Johanna led her away. Was he making a mistake letting them go? Any of them could have accessed the room, poisoned the tea, slipped in and murdered the Pope. He could imagine any number of motives – fear, devotion, greed. Someone could have paid one of them off to ensure the conclave never happened.

He could imagine, but he didn't know. Scribe IV was in over his head; he needed help, and quickly. Things were about to get much worse.

The moment the Drowned Sisters completed their ascent, they would lock down the Bastion. They would take over the investigation, in all likelihood delivering a verdict they'd decided on long before their arrival. At best, he and the rest of the staff would be exiled. But he doubted they would be let off that lightly. The Sisters were merciless, relentless. Creatures of nightmare with methods of extracting information and meting out punishment best left to archaic depictions of hell.

It was far more likely that he and all the human inhabitants of the Bastion would be Drowned.

He needed to find Dominic and learn what he'd seen.

He needed to get a message out of the Bastion.

The stairs rang with his steps, spiraling upward. Scribe IV burst through the door to his room. Above the jagged edge of stone, against the faint shimmer of the shield protecting the Bastion, clouds swirled and purpled and thickened, a rising storm. Below, the waves lashed to a frenzy, white froth pounding against the cliff with righteous fury. And beneath those waves, a terrible thing made its way toward the surface. Behemoth. Leviathan. Monstrosity. The Drowned Sisters' ship churning up from the deep, sloughing water, poised to burst forth and scream its presence to the sky.

Scribe IV slammed his fingers against the console without bothering to tune the communication band, throwing his message scattershot wide, and hoping somebody – anybody – would hear.

"To any unaffiliated investigator. There has been a murder. The Bastion needs your help immediately. Please respond. Please respond."

2

The pinging alert took an insistent hammer to Quin's dream, smashing it to pieces.

"Fuck off." He pulled the thin pillow over his head and folded it around his ears.

"Voice command not recognized."

"I said *fuck*... Never mind." Too late; he was awake.

He threw the pillow across the room and sat up, slapping the alert into a pillar of light projected from the table beside his bed.

"To any unaffiliated investigator..."

A surge of adrenaline shot through him. Quin was fully awake now. If he could scoop this job before anyone else...

He needed the credits, gods knew.

"... Bastion..."

The Bastion, where in days of old, gods were raised.

A ringing in his ears swept the rest of the message away. Something approaching panic gripped him, though he couldn't think why.

Where gods...

He shook himself, focusing. The message repeated, text scrolling around the image like a halo, a variety of languages spoken and written, morse code pulsing like a heartbeat. He squinted at the image in the light, the message's sender.

An automaton. An old-fashioned word for an old-fashioned model of synthetic being, but it fit. Its delicate face, a hammered mask of serenity polished to a high shine, a frame wrought like the bones of a human skeleton, revealing between them the delicate inner workings of crystals, wires and gears, couldn't belong to anything as crude as a bot. It had to be an automaton, a mechanical wonder from another time. A relic surpassed by other forms of AI, nanites and super-computers, but also lovely, made for the sake of beauty as much as efficiency. Not just a highly intelligent machine, but a creation meant to honor the gods. Or to mock them, depending who you asked.

Scribe IV. Quin read the designation and a tattered memory surfaced from the recesses of his mind. The case of a missing child who'd claimed sanctuary at the Bastion, maybe five, six years ago – hadn't he met a Scribe IV then? He'd been working steadily at the time, but not always sober. The details were hazy, a result of the pixie dust, or the simple ravages of time. Or—

Quin cut the last branch of thought off before it had a chance to bloom. He'd been clean three years now. Following that line any further would only bring the temptation to slip back into old habits. Bad ones.

He composed a hasty reply – his fee and the terms of his standard agreement – and fired it off.

The reply bounced, as if it had struck a wall. An attempted diagnostic brought a squall of sound – unsound – crawling up his jawbone, curling with loving brutality around the base of his skull, drawing headache tears to his eyes.

"The fuck?" Why call for help and then slam up a firewall blocking all replies?

Unless the signal jam came from elsewhere. Quin didn't need more than one guess at who that might be. The Sisters of the Deep, claiming whatever mystery lay in the Bastion for their own. Rumor had it they'd been after control of the Bastion for years. This – whatever it was – might just be the excuse they needed to seize it. Their justice would be swift and wouldn't look like justice at all to any eyes but their own.

"Fine. We'll do it the old-fashioned way." Because someone telling Quin not to only made him want to dig in harder.

Prayer, pure and simple. The surest way to get an angel's attention, to goad or compel them into action. And most importantly, a form of communication the Sisters couldn't lock down.

Quin set an incense cone to burn, and folded himself onto the floor, palms resting on his thighs, eyes closed. Once his prayer had been heard by the angels, it would also be conveyed to and recorded by the Bastion's Scribe. Not the most secure communication network, but Quin was aiming to be overheard. Who else but an automaton in a rotting outpost on the edge of a dying world even paid attention to prayers anymore?

Who else would be listening specifically for *his* prayers, except—

No. He wouldn't even let himself think it; he'd promised Lena.

Mind clear. Breath – in, out. Focus on intent. He didn't want to invite attention, only convey a message. Mind clear. Don't think about anything. Don't think about—

—*the chapel. Light oozing through scant cracks in the boards sealed over the window to keep*—

Breath – in, out, shallower now. Quin fought to bring it back under control. Ignoring the sweat prickling under his arms, panic wanting to rise like the Sisters' tolling, buzzing, crawling jamming signal that still echoed in his bones. Hold it together. Remember to breathe. Shut out the thud of his pulse and the—

—*aisle between the worn pews, knees bruised with supplication, palms together as in prayer, but the litany in his mind only* don't notice me, don't notice me, don't notice me, *lest the god of his father*—

Quin's eyes snapped open, his breath drawing incense unwittingly into his lungs, leading to violent coughing. His eyes watered for a different reason now, washing out the last memory of the Sisters' denial of his message. Washing out whatever else had tried to come through, tried to crawl up from the part of his mind that remembered his nightmares. Because that's all it had been. A nightmare. The images went skittering back into those dark corners, and Quin breathed out.

There was no way to know whether his prayer had gone through, or who else might be listening. All he could do was hope. A use for faith in a world of concrete proof, after all.

3

And in the echoing expanse of Heaven, bounded and boundless, Angel heard the desperate man's prayer. It left xem intrigued. A murder, in need of an investigator.

Angel unfolded. Xe had always been just Angel, with no need for any other name. Angel, fluid and ever-changing. Xe could be a private investigator. Why not?

A grin sketched the air, though Angel didn't have a face at that moment. In the blink of an eye – dozens of eyes in fact, of every conceivable color and some that were inconceivable as well – xe chose a new form. A meteor streaking through the vastness to Heaven's Ark Station and the desperate man at prayer. A prayer that was itself an echo of a desperate call for aid.

There has been a murder. The Bastion needs your help immediately. Please respond.

4

The sharp sound of shattering glass came from the dining hall above the kitchen, followed immediately by a muffled curse, and then shouting. Scribe IV's hearing was attuned enough to pick out Marius's voice, yelling at Seb, and the Cook yelling right back. In short order, the volume of their argument grew loud enough that despite the thick stone walls, the rest of the staff would surely hear them too.

Should he have ordered everyone to stay in their rooms? Would they have listened to him if he had? The urge struck Scribe IV to pinch the bridge of his polished nose – a human affectation, meant to banish a headache. The whole of the Bastion had become a headache as the Sisters rose, taking their time about it, prolonging the torture.

Whatever he felt, it was far worse for the human staff – eyes stung with tears, either from fear or the growing pressure in the air. Frayed tempers, shot nerves. He should intervene before the fight above escalated from hurled words and glasses to physical blows. But he still hadn't found Dominic yet. Or Agnetta, for that matter. Other than Seb, she was the most likely to know where the boy might be found. She was like a big sister to Dominic, knowing what it was like to be abandoned to the Bastion's care. They'd both been left at a young age, and had never known their birth families, so they'd become family to each other.

Scribe IV crossed the kitchen to the winding stairs leading to the pantries and cellars, leaving the sounds of the argument behind. Seb could take care of himself – and a small, weary part of Scribe IV didn't entirely mind the idea of the Head Butler taking a blow if it came to that. It was an uncharitable thought, a terrible dereliction of his duty, but at this precise moment, Scribe IV didn't care. Seb and Dominic did not treat him as a blasphemous thing; Marius did. The calculation was as simple as that.

Alcoves lined the walls of the spiraling stairs. A few still held carvings of the kind that had once filled the Bastion. The eeriest among them – which had once adorned the outer walls and since been moved inside – had limbs and faces long since eaten away by wind, time and salt. Dominic loved the statues – the more decayed, the better. Scribe IV had thought he might find the boy here, but it seemed increasingly likely that he'd fled to the cellars where he and Agnetta often played hide and seek.

At least, he hoped he would find Dominic there. Otherwise, he would have to descend all the way into the tunnels.

Scribe IV's footsteps wound him into the dark labyrinth of the cellars. Row upon row of sacred casks hulked against the walls. How many of them would have been tapped for the first time in thirty years if the Pope wasn't currently lying dead four floors above?

"Dominic?" He called the boy's name softly, not wanting to startle him.

A faint sound – the catch of breath, sniffling muffled too late. The figure half-crouched in front of the row of casks was too large to be the Page. Agnetta's head jerked around toward Scribe IV, dark curls framing a distraught face. Just beyond her, he caught sight of Dominic, folded small between two of the barrels.

"Dominic. Agnetta." Scribe IV made his voice as gentle as possible.

Both the Page and Chambermaid looked ready to bolt.

"Neither of you are in trouble," Scribe IV said. "I… when I couldn't find you, I became concerned."

A small lie. Not entirely a lie, even. Inasmuch as he could, he cared for Agnetta and Dominic. They looked stricken, shaken, and why shouldn't they be? On top of whatever Dominic had seen in the Pope's room – and Agnetta's fear for him – they would both be feeling the effects of the Sisters' rising by now.

Dominic released his breath, a wet sound, redolent of tears.

"This is a good hiding place," Scribe IV said.

Dominic didn't respond, his eyes wide as he looked from Scribe IV to Agnetta for reassurance.

Scribe IV had believed the Page to be at least twelve years old, but now he lowered his estimate. He'd always struggled with human age, especially when they were young. How old had Dominic been when he'd been left at the Bastion? How young had Agnetta been?

Scribe IV should know, but there were certain memories he found it easier to archive. Not forgotten, precisely, but put to one side. The excuse he gave himself was the freeing up of processing space, but in truth, the days on which children were left behind were always the ones he chose to download and put away. The haunted expression of those doing the leaving – the shame at not being able to care for children so vulnerable and young; their own hunger, which they struggled to hide; the low-banked fires of anger, of rage, at the world that had left them in this position.

It wasn't fair of him to forget, Scribe IV knew, but at times it felt necessary. It was always the same. Agnetta before Dominic, and Justine before her, a whole line of hollow-eyed, uncomprehending children left to the Bastion's care. His care. Had he done enough to protect them? Could he ever do enough?

He'd meant to question Dominic right away, but he couldn't bear to now – not when tears hovered in the boy's eyes, making him seem younger still. Dominic trembled, fought it, tried to be brave.

"Agnetta, would you please take Dominic back to his room?" Scribe IV asked.

"My duties, sir—"

The expression of alarm hadn't left Agnetta's face, as if she still expected to be chided. She looked like she wanted to flee; if it weren't for Dominic, Scribe IV suspected she would. How often did Anna-Maria berate Agnetta?

Once this business was over, he resolved to speak to her, perhaps remove Agnetta from her direct supervision. Anna-Maria wasn't kind. He should have done more to protect Agnetta and Dominic both. Perhaps he could at least do a small thing for them now.

"You're both excused from your duties for the rest of the day," he said.

Scribe IV turned his attention back to Dominic.

"Will you come out? Agnetta will take you upstairs. I'm sure Seb can spare a few more shortbreads to go with some of your favorite tea."

Scribe IV wished he could offer a reassuring smile. Agnetta did it in his place, holding out a hand to Dominic. But it shook. Tears shone in her eyes now too, though she fought them back as Dominic had.

"It's okay, little mouse." Agnetta's voice quavered on the nickname.

Scribe IV had not heard her use it in quite some time. It was a sign of his fear that Dominic did not protest that he was too old to be her little mouse anymore. He unfolded himself from between the casks. Before he could take Agnetta's hand, he winced, sucking in air audibly. He flinched, nearly doubling over, as if trying to duck away from something.

"It hurts," Dominic said.

He squeezed his eyes closed, his breath shallow. There was a fast, faint whistle to it. Now that the casks no longer shadowed him, Scribe IV saw flakes of rust-red around his nose, as if it had bled recently and been wiped away.

More evidence of the impact the Sisters' slow, torturous rise was having on the Bastion.

"Oh, mouse." Agnetta threw her arms around him. Dominic clung to her, letting himself shake.

The boy was small, whatever his actual age. There was a frailty to him – collarbones prominent, exhaustion and strain showing in blue-gray smudges beneath his dark brown eyes.

"I'm sorry, Dominic." Scribe IV put a hand on the boy's shoulder and left it there while Agnetta continued to hold him.

After a moment, Dominic drew back. His expression was miserable as he wiped at his cheeks. Scribe IV caught Agnetta surreptitiously doing the same. Dominic took her hand, and she fought to smile for him when he looked up at her. Dominic tentatively echoed the expression, both trying for the other's sake to be brave.

Scribe IV felt like he was intruding when he spoke. "Take care of each other. I'll come check on you both later."

Agnetta glanced back, just long enough to give Scribe IV a sharp nod, a jerky motion that betrayed strain. She kept a tight hold of Dominic's hand, as if she feared he would run away again, but Dominic pressed against her side. Scribe IV watched them cross the length of the room together, neither looking back at him, leaving him alone in the dim light as they climbed the stairs.

5

Prayer always left Quin achy, nervous, like an itch on the wrong side of his skin, one he'd never in a million years be able to scratch. If he was honest, it left him wanting a fix – a dangerous situation – but he'd promised Lena, and somehow, no matter how far away she was, his sister would know if he scored.

Besides, that wasn't a road Quin wanted to walk again, though the temptation was still there. He just hoped this job was worth it. Something in the plea, from the Bastion of all places, made him think he'd made the right choice. But the gut feeling didn't do anything to help with the pounding in his head.

Quin set his feet on the floor, feeling – he could swear – the cold metal through the station's thin carpeting. Like he swore sometimes he could feel the station's spin, even if the whole point of it was to simulate gravity and so it shouldn't be detectable at all. The room still smelled faintly of incense. He could taste it at the back of his throat, which had gone desert-dry while he napped.

There were tablets in his bedside table that would help with the headache. Quin paused with his hand on the drawer, the skin at the back of his neck and all along his spine prickling with the awareness of divinity.

Something in the dark, waking. Becoming, through the sheer power of faith, a god.

He slammed a door on the thought. Not even a thought; he wouldn't give it the dignity of acknowledging it as such. Just an artifact of the headache, like a migraine aura. He could almost convince himself that was true as he pushed himself to standing and clenched his jaw.

The terrible thing about prayers, Quin considered, bracing himself, was that sometimes gods answered. The door chimed, unnecessarily – he could already feel the pressure, the sense of waiting on the other side.

He briefly considered burrowing back under the covers, but it wouldn't do any good. The thing on the other side of the door had the patience of angels and wouldn't be leaving anytime soon. Quin palmed open the door.

As it turned out, a wheel made up of countless eyes and wings and fire and song could still somehow grin, and it was a very unsettling thing.

"Aquinas St. John?" The words weren't a question in the angel's mouth – mouths, none of which were visible – but the question mark was there nonetheless, an audible courtesy.

"Yeah?" Quin suppressed the urge to tack *who's asking* to the end of his reply. He felt a brief moment of relief, a brief moment of regret – he didn't recognize the angel at his door. He would never get used to this skin-prickling,

34

body-turned-inside-out sensation. Experience dealing with angels only made it worse. He knew what they could do.

But who knew what to expect from an angel as determinedly showy as this one? Eyes and wings and chiming song. Really? Why not a flaming sword? A chariot wheel tolling doom?

"You need to travel to the Bastion," the angel said. Xyr grin was no less self-satisfied the second time around. "I propose a partnership."

"I normally work alone. But..." Quin gripped the doorframe. The station's gravity seemed on the point of giving up.

He did need help. The Sisters would have the Bastion locked down in no time if they hadn't already. That wouldn't be a problem for the angel, and while xe didn't seem the wrathful type, turning xem down when xe'd made a perfectly reasonable offer would be rude at best, and – if Quin was wrong about xyr nature – downright unwise.

His bones creaked, the station's gravity shifting again. The sense of being on the verge of falling receded, and he relaxed his white-knuckled grip on the door. "But I could use a ride, and there's no harm in having more than one set of eyes on the case."

He immediately regretted his choice of words as the angel blinked and Quin lost count of how many sets of lids opened and closed. Gods, it sounded like a terrible pun. He forced himself to keep looking at the corridor-spanning wheel of fire and multi-colored eyes. The angel didn't seem offended. Maybe Heaven didn't do puns.

"Partners it is," Quin breathed. "But any chance you could tone it down?" He gestured to the spinning, chiming awfulness – in the truest sense of the word. "If we're going to work together, I'm not sure I can stand to keep looking at that. Fragile human mind, and all."

The angel shifted. The wheel of fire became something almost human, if Quin discounted the sheen of xyr skin, suggesting marble, the inky void of xyr pompadour, which contained the faintest glimmer of distant stars, and xyr eyes like smoked violet crystals, simultaneously whole and fracturing. At least there was only one set of them now. Xe'd put on clothes, but something told Quin it was more for the angel's own amusement than any sense of propriety. Xe wore a black leather jacket, rhinestone-studded leggings and heavy lace-up boots with thick soles that looked perfect for stomping. An outfit that belonged in the Ancient Earth media section of a museum.

Rowan had made him consume enough ancient movies over the years that Quin had developed an appreciation. Despite his better judgment, he grinned. "Perfect."

"Are you ready?" the angel asked.

Xe held out xyr hand. It took Quin a moment to remember he still wore only boxer shorts and the rumpled t-shirt he'd slept in, and that his feet were bare. His first instinct was to say *fuck it*.

"I'm certain Scribe IV wouldn't mind." The angel's smile was no less unsettling on lips that approximated human.

The ache between Quin's eyes deepened. Bloody angel, reading his mind. He took a moment to pinch the bridge of his nose. His doubts were growing by the moment, but it was too late to back out now. He grabbed the nearest thing to hand – gray sweatpants – and pulled them on, leaving the t-shirt as it was.

"Ready. Could you do me one more favor?" He met the angel's eyes. "If you're going to traipse around in here," he tapped the side of his head, "could you avoid rearranging or removing anything?"

There was genuine surprise in the angel's cracked-crystal eyes, as if xe found the very idea repulsive. The eavesdropping hadn't been conscious, Quin decided, only second nature, like breathing. It struck him that this angel was young, inasmuch as an angel could be young. Maybe inexperienced was a better word. Not every angel liked to wallow around in the muck of humanity. This angel might not have spent any time around humans before, might not know that most found having their thoughts read uncomfortable.

The angel's expression grew more solemn, almost pitying. Xe had absorbed in a flash, perhaps without even meaning to, all of Quin's history; had understood his first-hand experience with angels.

There were some people who got off on having angels mess around inside their brains. Quin didn't exactly count himself among their number; it was far more complicated than that. But even though he didn't want this angel inside his head, at the same time, the knowledge that what he knew, xe knew, left him strangely relieved. He didn't have to explain his skittishness at least. His unease over what a less scrupulous angel would do.

The angel lowered xyr head in a respectful gesture. An acknowledgment of Quin's past experience with xyr kind, an apology for xyr accidental trespass into his thoughts. Something turned over inside of Quin. He found himself liking this angel despite himself, some of his doubt melting away.

"I never would without permission," xe intoned.

"Yeah." Quin sighed. That was precisely the problem. "I know."

He put his hand in the angel's. Xe dissolved, dissolving Quin as well, turning him inside out for real this time, unraveling and unmaking him on the most fundamental level and screaming them through space to reassemble them both, unharmed, in the Bastion.

6

Scribe IV returned to his tower room and closed the door. Prayers awaited him. There was work to do, and he couldn't bring himself to approach any of it. At least Dominic and Agnetta were together, but were they safe? Were any of them in the Bastion safe?

A *whump* of displaced air buffeted him, bringing with it a scent like scorched ozone. A column of flame appeared and faded just as quickly to reveal an angel clad in leather and spandex, alongside a rumpled man in sweatpants and a t-shirt.

"Aquinas St. John," Scribe IV said.

When he'd sent out his desperate call, he'd wondered if it might find St. John still on Heaven's Ark, but he hadn't allowed himself too much hope. He allowed himself a little now, trying to put aside the fact that St. John answering his call in person meant that Scribe IV had put the man in danger.

"I apologize. I didn't think I would have company so soon," Scribe IV said.

He swept a dismayed gaze over the room. Bottles of ink that ought to be neatly replaced in racks and scrolls of paper that should be tucked away littered his desk. He couldn't even give himself the excuse of having left the room in a hurry. He'd picked up terrible habits from so long spent among humans; keeping a disorderly workspace was one of them.

"I tried to send a reply," St. John said.

He indicated the prayer scrolls that Scribe IV had not yet had time to review, but the gesture wobbled. His face had a queasy pallor, as though he might be sick.

"Angel." The angel stepped forward and held out xyr hand, looking pleased.

Scribe IV took it, inclining his head in a gesture of respect, noting as he did that Angel had given xemself chewed-short nails. St. John looked up, still unsteady. Scribe IV pulled over a chair, but the investigator merely braced himself against the back of it, gaping at the angel.

"Your name is Angel? You're an angel and your name is…" He trailed off, shaking his head.

"It suits me," Angel said.

"Of course it does," St. John said. He turned his attention back to Scribe IV. "And you and I, we do know each other, then?"

Human memory was so faulty. "You were here several years ago—"

"The missing boy."

"He became a god," Scribe IV confirmed.

"Right. His family thought he was a runaway, but he…"

40

St. John frowned as if he'd forgotten the word – or as if the word itself troubled him.

"Ascended," Scribe IV said. "May I offer you a drink, Mr. St. John?"

"Quin. A drink would be great. Thanks."

"Me too?" Angel asked. Xyr tone of hope, almost giddy, took Scribe IV by surprise, but he dutifully removed the stopper from the heavy cut-glass decanter of the scotch he kept for the rare instances when he had visitors and poured two measures.

Angel beamed as Scribe IV handed the glasses over. Xe lifted the glass and the liquid within caught fire. Delighted, Angel swallowed the flame whole.

Quin finally sat. He looked steadier now, but the worn expression remained. He'd aged since Scribe IV had seen him last, beyond the physical passing of years. When they'd found the soon-to-ascend child in the sea-hollowed caverns beneath the Bastion, instead of dragging the child back to his family and collecting his pay, Quin had readily accepted the boy's imminent godhood and let him go. Not many investigators would be so accommodating.

Scribe IV recalled the boy's beatific smile, the scent of warmed beeswax, which only that moment of divine intervention allowed him to smell, and the way the light clung to the child's brown skin and soft, dark curls. It wasn't long before he'd become too bright to look upon. Aquinas St. John's face in that moment of transcendence had been a mixture of melancholy, fear and wonder. It seemed to Scribe IV that the melancholy had remained, making itself a permanent part of Quin's features.

"So," Quin said, "there's been a murder."

"Yes," Scribe IV said.

The pressure of the Sisters' rising buzzed against his skin, but Quin and Angel were already here, and while he did have a healthy appreciation for mystery, sometimes the most satisfying thing about a mystery was knowing it could be solved.

"The Pope," Scribe IV said.

"Shit." Quin grimaced, sipping his drink, then gestured toward the oppressive sky above the tower. "And the Sisters have taken over the investigation, or they're about to."

"Indeed."

"Were there any witnesses? A motive? A murder weapon?" Angel asked.

Xe gripped the back of Quin's chair, holding xemself in place, doing a poor job of concealing xyr excitement. The idea of investigating a mystery clearly thrilled xem.

Scribe IV had once presumed angels to be omniscient. Now, he understood that they were constrained by certain rules. Those rules were capricious, like the gods themselves. Prayer could compel an angel to act, bind them, but they were afforded certain graces as well. They could, for instance, choose how much to know, when to know it, much as Scribe IV himself could put his memories aside. It was a matter of mercy – in both cases – as much as anything else. He'd heard of angels who'd cracked under the weight of knowing everything all at once. He wondered if Angel had been old at one time, and had chosen to become something new, or if xe was truly as young as xe seemed.

"There were no obvious wounds on the body. I couldn't immediately determine the cause of death. The Pope was holding a piece of paper in his hand, but it was blank." Scribe IV tried not to be discouraged as he catalogued the lack of information aloud. "The one thing we do have, however, is motive. The Pope came to the Bastion to propose that all organized religion be abolished."

"I suppose that would make a lot of people nervous," Quin said. "But nervous enough to kill?"

"That, I do not know." Scribe IV thought of Dominic's words about Johanna and her dislike of the Pope. All those keys left in the dark under the Bastion… Might they be prayers for the strength to do something awful? More likely, Scribe IV was letting his own biased opinion of the Chatelaine get in the way.

"There's one witness," Scribe IV added. "Dominic discovered the body. I don't know what else he might have seen. He's young, and he's terrified, but I believe we should question him before we run out—"

A bell tolled, cutting off Scribe IV's words. Not the rolling sound, like a swell building, that had first announced the Sisters' rising. This was sharper, a wave breaking. It made Scribe IV think of a wet finger dragged around the rim of a glass. A warning, purposefully delivered too late. Scribe IV hurried toward the ruined tower wall.

"Shit," Quin swore behind him, and Scribe IV turned to see blood pouring from his nose like an open faucet.

If frayed tempers and bloody noses were the worst of it, the humans of the Bastion could count themselves lucky. Scribe IV had heard of far worse occurring as a result of the Sisters' proximity – burst eardrums, blood clots. He'd heard of people not only fainting, but falling into comas from which they never woke after encountering the Sisters. He suspected at least some of the tales had grown in the telling, rumored horrors mixed with reality, which was bad enough.

"All persons present will remain inside the Bastion. Departure is not permissible. Failure to comply will be met with swift retribution."

The words came from everywhere. Whatever the Sisters had used to jam communications let them broadcast as well, voices clear from beneath the waves.

Scribe IV peered over the ruined wall. A figure pelted across the open, rocky ground toward the bay where the emergency shuttles were kept. From this high up, Scribe IV couldn't tell whether it was a member of the permanent staff, or one of the temporary workers hired for the conclave.

A wave smashed against the cliffside, but instead of falling back again the water whirled together to form a spout. The running figure skidded, trying to turn back toward the Bastion. The column of water swayed for a moment, sinuous and terrible, like the limb of some great sea beast. All at once, it fell – a lightning strike, pulverizing the fleeing worker. Bones snapped in an instant, flesh pulped into the ground. Scribe IV was thankful his hearing wasn't sharp enough to catch the sound from here, but that didn't stop him imagining it.

A damp, precise crater remained as the waterspout withdrew.

"This," the Sisters intoned, as a second, lower bell tolled like a mourning echo, "is our mercy."

How could they have known from beneath the waves? But then, they'd known about the Pope's murder. Perhaps, among the many stories Scribe IV had heard about the Sisters, the one that claimed their dreaming god whispered to them ceaselessly was true. He'd often wondered why anyone would swear to such a faith, how they could stand it. Maybe it was this, and the lightless depths that drove them to mete out such extreme punishments. Or were those who chose to follow the Drowned God already cruel, and that was what drew them to their strange worship in the first place?

"They... they shouldn't. They can't—" Angel had appeared beside him, leaning against the ruined wall, bitten nails gripping the stone. All xyr earlier glee had vanished, xyr expression stricken.

"I'm sorry," Scribe IV said. "If I'd realized..." If he'd prayed, would Angel have been able to intervene? Would the prayers of a machine even count?

If he prayed now, perhaps Angel could undo what had been done. "Could you—"

"No." Angel cut him off, the word in xyr mouth a sharp command.

There was enough force behind it that Scribe IV felt a physical hand placed against his chest, shoving him back, even though Angel hadn't touched him. Xe trembled, xyr eyes the purple-gray of a storm, sparked with lightning hidden within the clouds.

"I'm sorry," Scribe IV said again, chastised.

He understood without the angel telling him – preventing death was one thing, but turning it back would be something else altogether.

Angel blinked, xyr eyes clearing, though a fragment of doubt lingered. Quin joined them at the wall. Red spattered his shirt and smeared his skin, but the bleeding had stopped. His expression was grim as he looked over the edge of the wall.

"I guess we'd better work quickly."

Angel transported them to the corridor outside Dominic's room. The shorter hop seemed to have less effect on Quin, but he still looked queasy. Scribe IV considered the wisdom of introducing the already traumatized boy to a blood-stained man and an angel, but he needed a perspective other than his own.

"Dominic?" Scribe IV knocked softly.

A quiet response from within, and Scribe IV pushed open the door. A sliver of gray-green light showed through the window, but otherwise, the room was dark. Dominic sat up in his bed, knees tucked to his chest, arms wrapped around them.

"Where's Agnetta?" Scribe IV asked.

"She… went to get the tea from the kitchen, but she hasn't come back." Dominic looked uncertain, his gaze moving past Scribe IV to Angel and Quin.

"These are my friends," Scribe IV explained. He hoped it sounded reassuring.

He stepped further into the room, Angel and Quin

following him. "We'd like to ask you some questions, about what you saw in the Pope's room."

Dominic hugged his knees, expression still wary. Quin hung back, looking uncomfortable, but Angel drew closer. A faint glow radiated from xyr skin. Not enough to light the room, just enough to make the dark seem a little less.

"You don't have to be afraid, Dominic," xe said. "We only want to help. Are you able to tell us what you saw?"

"It was…" Dominic looked between all three of them again, his gaze not seeming to know where to rest. Finally, he settled on Scribe IV, something familiar. His small body trembled when he spoke again. "The crawling dark, sir. I saw the crawling dark."

Behind Scribe IV, Quin's breath made a strange hitching sound. Scribe IV turned as Quin took an unsteady step, as if the floor had suddenly tilted beneath him. Quin shook his head, a sharp motion, like trying to dislodge a fly from his skin, and braced a hand against the wall.

"Mr. St. John?"

Quin's breathing had become audible, panicked. Scribe IV took a step toward him, but Quin's head jerked up.

"I have to… I can't…" The sound of Quin's breathing worsened, color draining from his face.

A panic attack. He seemed on the verge of falling, but Angel caught and steadied him. Quin flinched at the touch, looking for a moment like he would strike Angel, before gathering himself, trying to regain a measure of calm. Scribe IV wondered if this was only the effects of being folded through space combined with the Sisters rising, or whether it was something else, something Dominic had said.

The crawling dark.

"I'll take him back to Heaven's Ark," Angel said.

"Go," Scribe IV agreed. "I'll stay with Dominic."

Space folded where Quin and Angel stood, there one moment, gone the next.

"Did I do something wrong?" Dominic asked.

"No. Mr. St. John is… ill. Is there anything else you can tell me, Dominic? When you say you saw the crawling dark, what exactly did you see?"

"It was like smoke, or a shadow," Dominic murmured, hesitant. "Only it moved fast. It crawled across the room, and then I couldn't see it anymore."

A demon might move like smoke – so might a cloud of insects. Flies gathered around corpses, but they were rarely the cause of death themselves. As a murder weapon, both seemed impractical.

"Was the Pope already lying on the floor when you went in, or did you see him fall? Did he say anything?" Scribe IV asked.

"He was already on the floor, sir."

"Did you hear or smell anything? Feel anything strange?"

"No, sir. I saw him there, and I saw the crawling dark, and I got scared."

"And there was no one else around?"

"Miss Anna-Maria was in the hall when I ran out of the room. She yelled at me to stop, and then she screamed," Dominic said.

He looked miserable. Scribe IV felt a measure of guilt

for putting the boy through this questioning. He'd already been through so much.

"Was it possible she was in the room before you?" he asked.

"I don't know, sir." Tears edged Dominic's voice, his distress audible.

Scribe IV couldn't help thinking that Angel would be better at this. That xe or Quin would think to ask something he had not. Perhaps he should have taken them to examine the Pope's body first, instead of bringing them here. Was he going about this all wrong? He didn't want to push Dominic too far, frighten him more than he was already, but he was also aware that they were running out of time.

"Why were you in the Pope's room, Dominic?" Scribe IV tried to ask the question as gently as possible.

The tears that had been hovering on the boy's lashes spilled over. "I went to get the tea tray, but I saw the crawling dark and the Pope, and I forgot. I'm sorry." Dominic buried his face against his knees, his shoulders shaking.

"You didn't do anything wrong, Dominic." Scribe IV hesitated a moment, then touched the boy's shoulder. He made sure to keep the touch light, but Dominic shuddered nonetheless. Scribe IV drew his hand away.

"You've been very helpful. Thank you," he said. "I'll go to the kitchen and see if I can find Agnetta. If not, I'll ask Seb to bring you the tea himself."

Dominic snuffled against his knees, but he didn't raise his head. It felt wrong, leaving him alone, but Scribe IV had no idea how to comfort him.

"Stay here," he said. "You'll be safe, and I'm sure Agnetta will be back soon."

He rose from the bed. The frame creaked, but Dominic didn't look up. Scribe IV hadn't been programmed for this. Weight clung to his metal bones, weariness and age he shouldn't be able to feel as he stepped back into the hall and shut the door behind him. He wanted to lean against the wall and rest, but a sound too small for what it portended sounded in the air.

Not a ringing this time, but a single chime, as of a hammer struck against the side of a bell, an eerie stillness falling in its wake.

Satisfied that they'd drawn out the torture long enough, the Sisters had finally arrived.

Scribe IV very much wanted to utter the curse that had occurred to him upon seeing the Pope's body, but he resisted the urge. He pushed away from the wall.

It was time to go outside.

Scribe IV made his way through the halls and exited by the cliffside door one level below the kitchen. The air felt changed, like a viscous oil coating his bones, one he would never be able to wash clean. Even he could taste it – sour brine and rotting seaweed slicking his throat.

He kept his attention fixed on the stairs. There was no rail guarding them, the drop beside him sheer. It was so rare for anyone to approach the Bastion from the water that the steps could afford to be wholly impractical. They were narrow, the color of rusted iron, the texture of basalt, scarcely wide enough for his feet – purpose-built to look foreboding.

The wind blowing off the water came heavily laden

with salt, but did nothing to dispel the rancid air. Even the sky looked wrong, less bruised-green now, more like something left to spoil. The delicate balancing mechanisms inside Scribe IV worked overtime. At least he didn't have the indignity of human lungs to leave him winded as he reached the bottom and made his way onto the rocky shore.

Other Bastion staff members had gathered on the beach, drawn by morbid curiosity, or perhaps fear that not appearing would be worse. The news would have spread, and by now, no doubt it had already been embellished. Wild rumors and conspiracy theories regarding the Pope's death, gossip instilling enough worry to make even the innocent uneasy and fearful of suspicion falling on them. Scribe IV caught Agnetta's eye, but she ducked her head immediately, perhaps feeling guilty for leaving Dominic alone. Her shoulders hitched; Seb stepped closer to her, putting an arm around her for comfort.

Marius was there, but Scribe IV didn't see Johanna or Anna-Maria. Did they have a reason to avoid the Sisters, or were they simply afraid? Judging by the miserable faces around him – more than one looking seasick as they huddled against each other – Scribe IV couldn't assign suspicion simply based on who had appeared on the beach and who had not. As much as he might wish he could.

Scribe IV stopped where the hissing tide hit his toes, watching the water heave and roil. There was one last unbearable moment of tension – then the leviathan broke the surface, waves curdling and sluicing from its hull. Metallic and organic, built and born, a gift to the Drowned Sisters of the Deep from their sleeping god. Or so they claimed. Limbs unfurled, thudding to the stony beach and dragging the creature halfway onto the shore. Its vast maw croaked open, disgorging a quartet of passengers.

Anglerfish.

It was the first word that came to Scribe IV's mind. Like the leviathan, the Sister leading the delegation seemed both organic and constructed. The protruding underbite of her jaw gleamed – metal and bone. In the center of her forehead, a light burned like a lure. Behind her, the three other Sisters arrayed themselves, heads not quite bowed, hands folded against their diving suits, which were more ceremonial than practical.

None wore gloves, revealing each had webbed fingers. Their heads were bare – two bore spiny, crest-like fins. One had eyes like lanterns. Each wore a chain around her neck, hanging almost to her waist, ending in a small bell.

Though he stood slightly ahead of the rest of the Bastion's staff, the Mother Superior didn't address Scribe IV in particular, but the whole beach. The same voice that had sounded out of the waves as the fleeing person was struck down, more muted now, resonated in his bones.

"The Bastion has been sealed and is now under the sole purview of the Sisters of the Drowned Deep. The investigation into the matter of His Holiness's untimely demise is ours. You will be informed when your assistance is required. Until such time, you are all remanded to your rooms, where you will remain until summoned. A strict curfew will be enforced. Anyone found in violation of these or any other orders issued by any Sister, at any time, will be Drowned."

7

At least an hour had passed since Angel returned Quin to Heaven's Ark. Quin sat on his bunk, feet braced against the floor, hands resting palm-down on his thighs, waiting for the hollow, inside-out feeling to recede. Breathing exercises hadn't done the trick. Panic edged ever closer.

He'd tried convincing himself it was the effects of Angel pulling him through space, and he'd failed.

The crawling dark – that's what the boy, Dominic, said he'd seen. Quin's mind had mercilessly filled in an image: darkness peeling away from the murdered body, crawling across the stone—

—*crawling, in the place where he didn't want to look, couldn't help but look*—

Memory, fighting its way back to Quin, whether he wanted it or not. Like something with too-long arms, slouching down the corridor outside his room. At any moment, it would scratch thick, black talons against his door, would break down the door if he refused to let it in.

Every time Quin took a breath to quell the anxiety, it got worse. Like the boy's words had kicked down a barrier in his mind, and finding a wound only superficially healed behind it, dug nails in, and ripped it open wide.

The bad thing wasn't coming for him. The bad thing was already here.

—light slicing sharp through the space between slatted wooden boards nailed over the windows.

The close, rank smell of the chapel. Something rotten. Something dead.

Hands clasped in prayer.

A quiet sob from close by.

Knees aching against the unforgiving floor.

And high up in the corner, just beneath the ceiling, a darkness that crawled and buzzed.

A darkness which shouldn't move, but did. Which opened its mouth and—

Quin slammed his hands against the bed, propelling himself to stand. He pulled on clothing more suitable for seeking out company, and splashed cold water on his face. He couldn't stay in his room. The – what could he even call them? Not dreams. He was wide awake. Visions? Hallucinations?

They were getting worse. More frequent. Chewing their way up from the depths of his consciousness. An ancient photograph, developing slowly. He didn't want to see the picture when it finally emerged.

He'd promised Lena he wouldn't fall back into old habits. Well, despite her lack of faith in him, he still had some capacity for self-control. He would go to see Rowan.

It had been months, after all, and whatever excuses Quin gave himself about being busy, he knew he'd been avoiding his friend out of selfish fear. He'd rectify that now. They'd talk, and Quin would do it all without scoring pixie dust to dull the feeling of something terrible drawing closer with every breath.

Besides, Rowan didn't even deal anymore. It was perfectly safe, just two friends sharing a drink – not a junkie and his faerie godmother. And if he was lucky, the crush and noise of the club might even be enough to hold the monsters at bay.

Candy-colored lights spun across the stage, following Rowan as he strutted, purred and growled his way through a song about heartache and revenge. Glints of pink, purple and blue dazzled off his platform heels, off the slinky-shivery gown cut down to his navel and slashed up to his thigh. Most of all, it caught on the gossamer wings at his back.

Quin settled in to wait. All the tables were packed, so he leaned up against the wall while Rowan sang one more song, then called a break, house music rising in his place.

As soon as he reached him, Rowan took Quin's hands and kissed him on either cheek, enveloping him in the scent of high-end face cream and powdered makeup.

"To what do I owe the pleasure?" he asked.

He led Quin to a reserved table. Quin watched, fascinated, as the clever mechanism of Rowan's wings folded themselves down to become another gauzy part of his dress.

"Social call?" Quin tried to make his expression disarming.

"Remind me to play poker against you sometime."

The server brought their drinks. The table was barely big enough to hold two glasses, and their knees crashed up against each other beneath it. Rowan had ordered something that glowed pale white; Quin hadn't paid attention to the name, telling the server to bring him the same. It tasted faintly of coconut.

"You're working a case," Rowan said.

"How can you tell?"

"Because you look like shit," Rowan said, but there was more worry in his voice than sting and he patted Quin's hand. "Drink up, and I'll order us another round."

Quin obeyed. By the time their second round arrived, Rowan was still watching him with barely veiled concern. "Have you been sleeping?"

"The perils of being folded through time and space," Quin said.

He offered a smile to soften the words, but Rowan's expression of alarm only grew. He'd meant it as a joke, so why the hell was Rowan so spooked? Unease prickled at the base of Quin's spine, suddenly on treacherous ground again. The thing slouching down the corridor had followed him here. He tried to redirect. "I didn't come to complain about work. It really is a social call. I miss you, even if Lena thinks you're a bad influence."

"Oh, I absolutely am, but I'm working toward being a good influence now, too. See?" An edge of doubt remained in Rowan's voice, but he dug around in the beaded clutch squished onto the curved bench between them and pulled out a token, tilting it so the cartoon devil printed on the side winked, growing a halo and a beaming smile as the light shifted over it. "Six months clean. I'm even working toward becoming a sponsor, so you can tell your pretty little sister not to worry. I won't corrupt your body anymore, just your mind."

Rowan pouted and blew a kiss. A tiny projector hidden somewhere in the sparkling fall of his chandelier earrings sent an animated lipstick mark fluttering through the air to land on Quin's cheek.

"Seriously, though." Rowan placed a ring-covered hand over Quin's on the table. "I'm here if you want to talk. I can blow off the rest of my set and we can do movies and popcorn, like the old days."

Rowan's warm, gorgeously manicured hand atop Quin's own unwound a measure of his panic, loosening his shoulders. Here, amidst the spinning lights and the gentle pulse of house music, the nightmares, the hallucinations, whatever they were, couldn't find him. Quin had the brief urge to rest his head on Rowan's shoulder and let himself drift off to sleep.

The idea that a bar teeming with people and noise felt like a safer and more peaceful place to sleep than his room made him uneasy all over again.

"Drinks first, and we'll see where the night takes us." Quin lifted his glass.

"Cheers, honey. To holding onto some vices, but not letting them hold onto us." Rowan clinked rims and downed half his drink in one swallow.

The watchful look didn't leave his eyes. Quin knew he was going to have to tell him something. Rowan's heart was bigger than anyone Quin knew. It would be fairer for Quin to give him something concrete to worry about than to let him imagine the worst.

It wasn't as though Rowan would judge him. He'd already seen Quin at his lowest. Hell, the first time they'd met, it was only because Quin accidentally stumbled into Rowan's dressing room, utterly fucked on pixie dust's dirtier cousin, pookah. He'd gotten lost looking for the bathroom. Back then, Quin scored from less scrupulous dealers who cut their dust with arcane shit, designed to hurt, which had been part of the point. He'd wanted to make a mistake. Rowan – whatever Lena's opinion of him – had been a blessing in disguise. His faerie godmother, his dealer, his savior.

He'd taught Quin to appreciate the smoother, cleaner high of pixie. And he'd steered him away from divinity – the all-too-human attempt to recreate the ecstasy and terror gifted by angels.

It had been Rowan's guidance that had allowed Quin to take the first step in turning his life around. The second step had been far less pleasant. Lena had literally tied him to his bed where he sweated and screamed and vomited his addiction out. She refused to leave his side no matter how much of a mess he made, or how much abuse he flung at her in his delirium.

Family was one kind of healing, but friendship was another. Rowan had been exactly what Quin needed. Without his intervention, Lena's harsher methods wouldn't have taken hold.

Even fucked out of his mind that first night, Quin had liked Rowan immediately. He'd stood gaping in Rowan's doorway, trying to work out whether Rowan was literally a vision, or just metaphorically. A pale violet wig, all glorious curls and glittering pins holding a gravity-defying coif in place atop the mannequin head on Rowan's dressing table. Rowan himself wore a stocking cap over his hair, his brows blocked and re-sketched higher up, the space beneath them drenched in glorious color, lips drawn into a shimmering bow.

He could easily have been pissy about the strung-out asshole blundering into his dressing room, and he would have had every right. But he hadn't missed a beat as Quin stood there swaying, pupils blown wide. He winked at Quin in the mirror and lifted a star-topped wand from the dressing table, waving it in a circle before tapping it against his own chest as he gleefully recited the magic words, "Bippity, boppity, boobs!"

"What?" Quin had replied stupidly, watching whatever enhancement Rowan had triggered fill in the cleavage beneath his shimmering, ice-colored ballgown.

"*Cinderella*." Rowan tsked, disappointed. "Don't you know your classics?"

Quin admitted he didn't, and later that night, Rowan had introduced him to the first of several versions of the movie they'd watch together over the coming days – enhanced by the steady flow of pixie Rowan provided. Quin had been starting to come down by the time Rowan's set ended, but back in his room, Quin's faerie godmother insisted on getting him high all over again after Quin explained that his name was not, in fact, short for Quinten.

"Your name is Aquinas St. John? Seriously? Oh, honey, you definitely need what I'm selling, and the first hit is absolutely on me."

Quin twisted the stem of his glass, debating how much to tell Rowan now. He trusted Rowan implicitly, and it wasn't a one-way street. They'd seen each other at their lowest, and occasionally brought each other to those lows by enabling bad decisions. But they'd grown together, too. Quin had done his fair share of saving Rowan's ass, and not as a way to return the favor. Dealer or not, Rowan was good, too good. He deserved saving.

Quin had thrown more than one punch on Rowan's behalf, and taken more than one too. Despite Rowan's height, his size and solid build, he was no fighter. Clients who took issue with Rowan's price structure, the supplier who'd tried to cut Rowan out of the process altogether... all had to answer to Quin. He'd seen Rowan through disastrous breakups and had literally been his left-hand man after shoulder surgery to correct a childhood injury which had never healed right, because back then, Rowan's family had to choose between feeding their children and adequate medical care.

So it wasn't judgment he feared. At least, not Rowan's. His own, maybe. He wanted Rowan to think the best of him, wanted to deserve his friendship. He wanted his faerie godmother to see the magic had worked and Quin wasn't some jittering mess in need of fixing. Not anymore.

The sugar from the drink left a slick coating on his teeth and tongue, and it occurred to Quin that he should have eaten something before starting on the alcohol.

"Have you ever heard of people experiencing… flashbacks from pixie, even after getting clean?" Quin asked.

He kept his gaze fixed on his glass, feeling his way into the conversation. His shoulders tightened reflexively, bracing for Rowan's answer. He wanted a rational explanation, a safe one. Anything that would allow him to sidestep the truth. Not dreams, not hallucinations. Memories.

"Have you been seeing dancing sprites?" Rowan asked.

His tone was light, but Quin didn't miss the edge beneath it.

Quin looked away, too late. What were eyes but a window to the soul? And apparently he was doing a shit job of keeping the blinds drawn.

The crawling dark.

"No, I've never heard of anyone experiencing a side effect like that." Rowan's tone was more serious now, his hand returning to cover Quin's. He blinked down the holo-lenses silvering his irises, leaving only their natural warm brown – the color of strong tea, flecked in the left eye with a single freckle of gold.

Quin had a sudden sense of foreboding. Rowan teasing, Rowan sarcastic, Rowan throwing shade – all of that he could handle. Rowan with a look like heartbreak in his eyes? The way he looked at Quin now – what did he know that Quin didn't know? That he'd forgotten?

"I know you don't want to hear this, but messing with Starling again isn't—"

Quin stopped listening, stopped being able to hear Rowan at all over the rush of blood in his ears.

Starling.

The name dropped the ground out from under him.

"Starling's here? You've seen him?"

"You haven't—shit." Rowan clapped a hand over his bright painted lips. "I thought when you said you'd been folded that you'd been traveling with him, or at least been to see him again."

"Different angel."

Quin felt numb. A hollow space opened up in his chest. Of course Starling was back on the station. Hadn't part of him known? When he'd prayed, hadn't he hoped, just a little bit, that this was exactly what would happen?

Rowan squeezed his hand. "Quin?"

He came back to himself to see Rowan once more peering at him with concern.

Starling. One of his many names, including Legion and Swarm. But never to Quin. To Quin, he was always Murmuration. His angel.

"Don't faint on me." Rowan's hand on his became fingers circling Quin's wrist.

Quin made his other hand release the edge of the table; he'd been gripping it until his knuckles turned white. If Rowan thought he'd been to see Murmuration, that meant—

Not hallucinations. Memories.

Memories he'd already tried to feed to his angel. And Rowan knew. Because they'd had this conversation – some version of it – before. He knew whatever it was Quin had forgotten. What he'd forgotten even the forgetting of, under his angel's ministrations. But obviously it hadn't taken, because here was the dark, surfacing, pressing like hands against the wrong side of his skin, trying to break free.

"Whoa. Easy." Rowan stood, catching the drink Quin had nearly tipped over when he lurched to his feet.

"I'm good," Quin said.

He tried to believe it, but his words returned to him, limned with a faint hum as if sounding from the far end of a tunnel.

"I'm sorry, I never should have—" Rowan began, but Quin held up a hand to interrupt him.

"It's not your fault, and I'm fine, really, just tired." He made himself meet Rowan's eyes, putting all the conviction he could into his tone. "I just need to go back to my room and lie down."

Rowan didn't look satisfied, but he did let go.

"I trust you, but promise you'll call me if things get too..." Rowan waved his hand. His nails sparkled under the lights.

Quin forced himself not to look away, and made his mouth approximate something like a smile. He didn't deserve Rowan's trust, not right now.

"I promise," Quin said. "Now get back up there. You have ravening fans waiting."

Rowan hesitated a moment longer, then dropped a kiss on Quin's cheek.

"I'll be standing by, ready to slay after I slay, so don't hesitate, okay?"

"I won't," Quin said.

The worry in Rowan's eyes dug at him. If he didn't deserve Rowan's trust, he certainly didn't deserve his kindness either. It was a relief when he turned away, striding back to the stage, crowd parting for him, wings unfurling. Quin didn't stay long enough to hear the start of the next song. His pulse thumped loud enough to drown out the music anyway.

Murmuration.

He shouldn't, but he would.

Quin allowed himself to be pulled like a body falling into a gravity well, straight toward where he knew his angel would be waiting.

8

Angel returned to the Bastion and found Scribe IV in his tower room, under the watery-green glow of the sky.

"I promise you, the Sisters can't detect my movements," Angel said, hoping to reassure Scribe IV, who looked startled. "And if they could, I sincerely doubt even their Mother Superior would be willing to risk the wrath of an angel."

Xe grinned, another attempt to put Scribe IV at ease, but he did not look reassured.

In truth, Angel couldn't blame him. Xe didn't know what the Sisters would risk. They'd called a waterspout to kill a frightened human trying to flee. They'd threatened the entire Bastion with Drowning. Drowning wasn't meant to be a punishment; it was a holy act. If the Sisters were willing to pervert it so, that meant they no longer spoke with the voice of their slumbering god. It was possible they had not done so for quite some time.

"Is Mr. St. John well?" Scribe IV asked.

He moved to pour Angel a measure of scotch.

"He's safely back on the station," Angel said.

It wasn't a full answer, but Aquinas St. John's secrets weren't xyr's to tell. And, if xe was being wholly honest with xemself, xe didn't want to share what little xe knew for selfish reasons as well.

Xe'd felt the shadow haunting Quin – fragments accidentally gleaned from his mind. Some of what troubled Quin was related directly to interactions with one of xyr own kind. Angel wanted Scribe IV to like xem, not put it into his mind that close association with an angel was a painful thing.

Xe also wanted to be *worthy* of being liked, to not be or become a dangerous thing that ought to be feared. The faint tug xe'd felt earlier lingered, when the fleeing worker had been killed, and Scribe IV had nearly asked xem to intervene. For the briefest of moments, xe'd felt a stirring far below the waves, below even the depths that the Drowned Sisters had plumbed. Something had called to xem, and xe'd been tempted to respond.

Angel pushed the thoughts away.

"Was Dominic able to tell you anything more?" xe asked.

"I'm afraid not," Scribe IV said. "And the Sisters have taken custody of the Pope's body, at least for now, so you won't have the opportunity to examine it yourself."

"I could, if I wanted to," Angel said. In fact, xe would enjoy circumventing the Sisters' rules, however that would likely make Scribe IV even more uncomfortable, so xe went on. "But I trust your assessment of the Pope's condition when you found him. Motive, then. Do you believe the Pope was killed because of his intention to propose the abolition of organized religion?"

Angel lifted xyr glass, let the alcohol within catch alight before sipping, fire rolling across xyr tongue.

"Perhaps so," Scribe IV said. "Many people would lose their jobs, have their entire lives upended. Not just the invited members of the conclave, but countless people in their flocks, their congregations. Even the Bastion and its staff would be impacted, myself included." Scribe IV couldn't smile, but Angel suspected he was trying to make a self-deprecating joke.

"The Bastion would no longer have an official purpose. We would have nowhere to go," he continued. "I would like to believe that no one on my staff is capable of murder, however the possibility cannot be ruled out. Am I clouding matters if I hold onto that belief?"

"You fear you cannot be impartial."

"It's why I asked for help," Scribe IV replied.

"But you don't wish to remove yourself from the investigation entirely." Angel leaned over the lowest broken section of tower wall, peering down at the crashing waves. The Sisters' leviathan was half-beached, bronze and verdigris, sinew and bone washed by the restless tide. It looked infinitely ancient and infinitely patient, though Angel knew – despite their claims otherwise – that the Sisters' presence below the Bastion was relatively recent as the scale of history went.

"The gods have never been the purview of any one church, temple, synagogue or otherwise. They have always belonged to themselves," Angel said. "If the Pope's views did get him killed, then I fear he died for nothing."

Xe hopped up onto the broken section of wall. Being in motion made xem feel better. Scribe IV made a sound of disapproval, and Angel held xyr arms out with exaggerated care to reassure him. As if gravity even applied to angels.

The moons had already passed their highest point in the sky and started their descent. The falling light was lovely. Xe could have happily remained contemplating it until the moons reached the horizon, but xe felt Scribe IV's restlessness. Time was a strange thing – a very human way of viewing the world. But Angel understood Scribe IV's sense of urgency, contemplating what their next step should be as xe paced the wall.

On the way back to the Bastion, xe'd made xyr appearance younger – frame narrower, feet bare, cheekbones less severe, eyes no longer like smoked glass. It had suited xyr whim in the moment, but perhaps xyr new aspect made Scribe IV feel protective, the way he seemed to feel toward Dominic.

It warmed Angel; the idea of someone caring for xem was appealing.

The sleeves of xyr jacket now overlapped the bones of xyr wrists, slipping halfway over xyr hands as xe scrambled up another section of wall. Xe reached the highest remaining point of the crumbled tower wall and executed a neat pirouette, dropping into a gargoyle crouch to peer down at Scribe IV. His polished eyes gleamed green with the light. He looked like he wanted to chide Angel and tell xem to get down from there, like a fretting parent. It only made Angel's grin wider.

"What do we know about the Pope, beyond his office?" Angel asked. Xe splayed xyr fingers over the edge of the wall, knees jutting up sharply on either side of xyr body. Xe could maintain this pose infinitely if needed, long past when the Bastion would crumble to dust and the land was reclaimed by the sea. But xe took pity on Scribe IV, shifting to sit with xyr legs dangling back into the tower room, hands braced comfortably beside xem.

"He came from a wealthy family," Scribe IV said. "The family made their fortune in mining on Hephaestus, and the Pope was something of an aberration among them. I believe he was truly faithful, but there were also rumors that his title was purchased, perhaps in an effort to lend his family a sheen of respectability, and to give them some degree of immunity regarding their less scrupulous business practices."

"If his family did purchase his title," Angel said, "perhaps they also arranged his death? Better to have him die a martyr than to abdicate his position?"

"It's possible." Scribe IV sounded melancholy. Curiosity made Angel change xyr line of questioning. The mystery of the Pope remained, but Scribe IV himself was a mystery as well.

"Why are you here?"

The question seemed to catch him off guard. "I was assigned."

"When?" Angel kicked xyr feet against the stone.

Angel knew Scribe IV's recall was instant; he didn't need to gather his thoughts before answering. He was stalling, trying to work out the motive behind xyr questions.

"During the rule of Her Holiness Lisbeth III."

"Over a hundred years now. Why do you stay?"

"I..." Scribe IV faltered, a hitch, as if one of the crystalline processing units inside him had developed a minute flaw.

"I like it here," Scribe IV answered at last. "It... feels like a place I belong."

"You remember it in its glory days."

"The Bastion used to be a haven for pilgrims," Scribe IV said. "Rituals of all kinds were observed in the gardens and in the caverns above the sea – some kind, and some cruel. The Twinned God sang a flight of angels from the sky, then cast them into the waters. Mortals were raised up to saints and gods. Miracles of all sorts took place here, along with the open exchange of ideas and discourse. Now, it is largely forgotten."

"And you feel a kinship with the Bastion?" Angel leaned forward slightly.

"Yes." Scribe IV's voice grew quieter. "We both belong to another age."

"Where else would you go?" Angel asked. "If you weren't this, what would you be?"

"I don't understand."

"Do you wish to be unmade? Or remade? Do you wish to evolve?"

The questions were dangerous. All the years of prayers

layered into these walls, the gods that had walked here, the angels that had fallen... Angel felt the weight of all that faith. It might not even require a specific prayer. Xe could do what xe had offered. Unmake Scribe IV. Remake him.

The realization should have been more startling. There were angels who never left the bounds of Heaven because the temptation to tap into this raw power, the very threads of creation, was too great. There were angels who chose to remake themselves for fear of what they might do.

Angel felt a stirring deep beneath the waves again. *Possibility. Power.* The knowledge that xe could change into something vast, if xe allowed xemself. The knowledge that perhaps, xe had already changed before.

It was an uncomfortable feeling. Xe'd seen glimpses in Quin St. John's mind of what an angel could do, of what they might become. Angel shuddered, pulling back into xemself, pulling away from the ragged edges of history xe felt in the Bastion's stones. Xe'd only wanted to help Scribe IV better understand himself, see that he could become more than his programming if he so desired.

A glimmer of something that might be alarm, or hope, or both, flashed in Scribe IV's eyes. This was a thing Scribe IV might have considered privately, but never out loud, and Angel had plucked it from the air and offered it to him.

"You could..." Scribe IV did not finish the thought.

"I could," Angel agreed – softly now, less certainty in xyr voice.

Xe'd been proud of xemself, rooting out something in Scribe IV that he'd never acknowledged aloud before.

Xe'd been having fun. And xe'd been careless. But now that xe'd drawn Scribe IV's attention to the possibility, xe couldn't lie about its existence either.

"If you wished. If you truly believe yourself to be obsolete. If you are unhappy, you could become something other than you are. I could help."

Xe watched contemplation slide like light over Scribe IV's polished features. It wasn't xyr place to impose any sort of decision, only present options. That was all xe'd done, wasn't it? Xe hadn't pushed Scribe IV to change his nature, only shown him that he could.

Angel understood how some gods could grow addicted to prayer, how they could gorge themselves on human desire, and how, in the great turning of existence, many had gone mad with it.

"I will think on it." Scribe IV bowed his head in gratitude.

"Good." Angel pushed the unease away, turning xyr mind back to the problem of the Pope. "I want to search the grounds," xe said. "Starting with that structure."

"The labyrinth ruins?" Scribe IV looked where xe'd indicated. "Why?"

"If I were human, I would call it a hunch." Xe let mischief slide across xyr expression.

Angel pushed xemself off from the wall. Scribe IV gave a flinch and a half-step, as if he meant to catch xem before remembering himself. Angel landed neatly, xyr feet making no sound.

"Aren't you curious about what we might find?" Angel asked.

"I suppose." It was a grumbling admission, but Angel knew the truth – no mind-reading required.

Scribe IV valued mystery as much as xe did.

"Good. Then you can come with me. Satisfy my curiosity. I promise to keep you safe from the Sisters' prying eyes."

Angel held out xyr hand. Scribe IV barely hesitated before taking it. Quick as a thought, xe folded them inside out, stealing Scribe IV away from the Bastion and down into the ruined garden high above the crashing sea.

9

Quin moved deeper into the station's leisure district. Back in his room, something crouched, lurking, waiting for him. It folded too-long legs against its chest, gnawing on the claws that had dragged against the floor as it slunk and stalked him.

Quin couldn't go back there. Not alone.

Dante's Inferno. Quin wedged himself into the already packed club, shouting above the pulse-bass-thump of music to get the bartender's attention. Like its unsubtle name, the club screamed excess. Three levels of premium station space crammed with platforms and cages, catwalks and swings. Bodies gyrated and writhed on or in or dangled from every single one of them, slicked in glitter and sweat, spit and cum. All of it washed persistently in strobe lights that only made Quin's headache worse.

He regretted not getting high, despite his promises to Lena. Even sober, everything fractured and stuttered in the light; bodies twisted and elongated and became improbable, almost inhuman.

Quin leaned as far over the blue-lit bar as he could and shouted to the bartender again – a very cute person with a shaved head and kohl-lined eyes.

"What can I get you?" Their words buzzed with the music; Quin read their lips as much as heard their voice.

"Have you seen…" The blood-beat bone-crunch of sound stole Quin's attempt at an explanation. What name would Murmuration even be going by now?

"What?" The bartender scrubbed a glass which refused to look any cleaner.

"Birds?" It came out as a question, despite Quin's best efforts. *Pathetic.* "Shadows?"

He tried to describe a shape in the air with his hands, and failed. He might as well be high for all the sense he wasn't making. He took a deep breath and gathered himself.

"An angel. He might be here. He's my…"

He let the words trail, throwing the bartender a pleading look. It was hard to explain, not that the bartender was entitled to an explanation of what Quin and Murmuration had been to each other, what they might be again if he continued down this path.

Ex was too simple a word for it. Confessor? Tormentor? Quin could barely explain it to himself. Murmuration had disassembled him, taken him down to his base elements, stripped him to his soul and scoured that for memories to devour. And Quin had let him, invited the angel to rummage in the deepest parts of him, not just once, but many times. He'd given himself the excuse that he did it in exchange for information, things only an angel might be able to find out that had helped him solve more than one case.

"Spooky-looking motherfucker? Over there." The bartender hooked a thumb; Quin followed the gesture to a clustering of shadows on the far side of the club, skin crawling in a response more primal and more complex than simple desire or fear.

He authorized credit to the bartender's tip jar without buying one of the overpriced drinks. Despite his longing, he knew he should be sober for this. Or as sober as possible, at least.

Crossing the floor felt like swimming upstream. Hands grasped at his shoulders, cupped and squeezed his ass and cock. Entering Dante's Inferno was as good as consent to some. Glitter smeared Quin's clothes by the time he emerged on the other side of the room.

There. Waiting, smug, knowing Quin would come looking for him eventually. Quin hated him, and his entire body sparked alight with desire.

Quin remembered – had forgotten, needed to be reminded every single time: looking at Murmuration could be like seeing overlapping layers of reality. Seeing more than one truth at one time, all equally weighted. A flock of birds. A swarm of shadows. A tall, pale man with long fingers, long black hair, eyes that devoured the light.

An illustration of an angel of old, surrounded by dozens and dozens of wings, a flock of birds in constant, restless motion, a creature with black talons tipping its fingers instead of nails, and needle-teeth.

Quin blinked, and the edges of Murmuration's being stopped shivering, became something that approximated human – a terribly beautiful and beautifully terrible man seated at a small table with just enough room for Quin to join him, two drinks ready and waiting, and perhaps most incongruous of all in this place, a small tealight candle flickering between them.

Murmuration gestured, a fluid motion of his long-fingered hand, and Quin sat. Sitting, in fact, became a necessity, Quin's legs boneless and incapable of supporting him. He tucked himself into place beside the angel and remained pinned there by Murmuration's smile.

"It's been too long." Murmuration leaned in, lips brushing Quin's jawline, a gesture familiar and frightening, one that didn't await permission, but claimed it as a right.

It was over so swiftly, Murmuration folded back so neatly – almost primly – into his own space that Quin couldn't be certain the angel had moved at all.

Had it been Dante's Inferno where they'd first met? Quin had been drinking alone, he remembered that much, when he'd felt a presence just behind him, taking up far more space than it rightfully should. A voice at his ear that was somehow also a hand at the base of his spine, an electric jolt of desire straight to his cock and to somewhere else, more fundamental than any physical part of his being.

"Be not afraid. We are Legion. We would very much like to buy you a drink and then fuck you."

It was the strangest pick-up line Quin had ever heard, and possibly the worst, but it had worked. He'd never met an angel before, had no idea what they could do, and he was at a low enough point that he didn't care. He'd simply thrown himself at eyes dark as infinity, and let Murmuration take him outside of himself.

But only physically, that first night at least. Everything else – the memory-eating, the help with his cases, the thing very much like addiction that Lena had sweated out of him along with the actual drugs – all of that had come later.

And now he found himself falling right back into Murmuration, as if he'd never gotten out, wanting and needing to be taken apart, flensed and scraped to the bone to escape the terrible thing in his head. Murmuration watched him, predator-patient, leaning back, simultaneously taking up all the space at their table and none at all.

"I need…" Quin started, and words failed him. He felt like a junkie all over again, only sheer force of will keeping him from trembling, jaw clenched, a shake starting somewhere at the center of his being and threatening to overtake him.

"I need…" Help. The case. Murder. The crawling dark. But he couldn't explain any of that aloud.

Murmuration leaned close again, cupped Quin's jaw – tender and hungry, comforting and awful. He spoke his answer against Quin's mouth, dissolving the world around them as he did and materializing them back in Quin's room, straddling Quin and holding him down, mouth still on his and hand still on Quin's jaw.

"I know."

The memory is ragged, edges chewed, all the more painful for having been regrown countless times, stronger and more stubborn with each return, no matter how often it is devoured.

Quin's knees ache, pressed to a hard wooden floor. His hands are bound, clasped palm to palm, rough fibers and the nodules of rosary beads digging into his flesh. Light seeps through the gaps between boards nailed over the window, sick and bright. His breathing is very loud, tear-wet and choked.

He is inside the moment.

He is outside the moment. It is only a memory.

He is inside his flesh, hundreds of thousands of miles and many years away.

He is inside his flesh, and he is not alone.

His angel is here.

The memory is a skein of thread the color of blood unwound from the core of him.

In the dark, something buzzes, it hums. It moves, though it no longer breathes.

Lena is with him. Too small, too fragile. She shouldn't have to see this. No one should have to see this. He wants to tell her to cover her eyes. He wants to cover his own, but his hands are bound and so are hers, and there is nothing he can do to comfort her.

Tears drip from his nose, from the point of his chin.

"This is love," their father tells them. "Perfect love. Perfect faith. This is how we will make a god."

Quin hears the words in his room on the station as his angel digs nails made from the stuff of existence into his flesh, pulling the words out of him again. Words that step across his skin, along the curve of his ear, like the feet of a fly. Not one fly, but a dozen, a hundred, clustered in the corner of the room, where he doesn't want to look, where he can't help looking. Where the man—

Time slips, a thread unwound and re-wound again before being snapped.

"This is love," his father says. "Faith alone is not enough. Gods require love, and you will love your god before the end. Your love will feed Him. When all else is stripped away, when fear has eaten everything else from you, you will worship Him, because you will know then that He is the only thing that can save you. He is the only way you can be free."

"No!" Quin shouts the word, maybe then, maybe now, but it changes nothing.

Time slips again, runs backward. Before the chapel, in the barn, his father leads a starved man picked up from the side of the road by a rope tied to his waist.

"Watch," he tells Quin and Lena, light burning in his eyes. "This is how gods are born."

He anoints the man's skin, washes his feet, sobbing prayers.

"My faith isn't enough," he tells Quin, tears unable to quench the fire burning and burning in him. "It has to be your sister. It has to be you. Don't look away."

He makes them watch as he plies the knife with loving kindness, each cut a prayer. He makes them watch as he twists the man's head back and whispers in his ear.

"You will become so much more."

Another stutter, another thread pulled, snapped. They are in the chapel. Their father binds their hands. He binds the man as well, like a spider's prey, tucked up below the ceiling. He nails boards over the windows and the door. He leaves Quin and Lena in the stinking dark with the dead man, the smell growing worse every minute, every day. He tells them to love their god and to pray.

Time lurches forward, then crawls. How long have they been in the chapel? An eternity.

Quin is dizzy with hunger, hollow and fever-hot. Lena slumps on the dusty floor beside him, her breath shallow. Unconscious – a mercy – but still alive. He will follow her soon. If he falls, will he have enough strength to catch himself with his bound hands, or will he smash his face into the floor? He tastes blood at the back of his throat. It has already happened. He is already—

Falling. Fighting not to fall.

This isn't love, a voice insists. Quin's voice? Someone else's?

His father is sick. He needs help.

No.

Quin needs help.

He will not love his father's god. He will not look. He does not believe.

The man is dead. He is a corpse, not a god. Buzzing, terrible darkness crawls across the man's body until that crawling dark is all Quin can see.

The flies walk across his skin instead of the man's. Is he hallucinating? Each step is a word, the voice in his head commanding him – *Turn your gaze upon me*.

Quin fights it, but he cannot fight for long. He is hungry, he is tired. It hurts so much, and he just wants it to stop. He looks where he does not want to look. He does not want to believe, but—

Above him, the dark buzzes and crawls. The air is hot and thick. Dust. Rot. A hundred thousand wings beat and trembling bodies feast. And—

The memory stutters, teeth-torn, shredded, by long-fingered hands on his chest, then sinking between his ribs, inside his skin. The most intimate touch of all – his angel rummaging around inside him, picking the memories clean, leaving him hollow.

The smell of the chapel. The taste of death, thick and clotted in the air. Wanting to die. Wanting it to end.

The promise in his mind that if he prays, it will. If he believes, if he loves his father's god, he will be free.

"I—" Quin says.

And the god, the crawling dark mass beneath the ceiling, shifts, opens its eyes, opens its mouth and speaks a holy word.

Quin screams. The word sears through him, through every layer of his flesh and bone, leaving a dark, ragged hole in his chest. He is still screaming now. He has always been screaming.

The sound pours from him with the thread of memory. Unwound from his heart and gathered in the angel's hands.

Murmuration arches above him, glutted and full. The memory is a shadow between his teeth, swallowed down like slick oil.

Murmuration is inside him, is him. And then his angel is a thousand, thousand beaks and claws and wings. A swarm, a legion. A murmuration filling every inch of space in Quin's room, swallowing and suffocating every bit of light.

A shuddering gasp. Quin falls into blissful unknowing, spent. The last thing he hears, does not hear, as every terrible thing spools away from him, is an echoing cry that could be pleasure or pain, both or neither, nothing at all.

Quin woke with the covers stripped off his naked body, not shivering, but on the cusp of it. The not-quite-tangible sensation of sweat dried to something tiny and crystalline coated his skin. Post-fuck sore. Stretched thin, headachy like a hangover, regret seeping in to fill all the empty spaces the moment he opened his eyes.

He'd made a terrible mistake. He'd been sober, clean, quit of the angel, but last night, he'd gone back. Why?

Feathers stuck to his pillow, tucking themselves into the folds of his sheets. The quill of one poked him in the back, and he imagined the veins of it imprinting themselves on his skin. Murmuration crouched on the chair next to the tiny desk that was the only other real piece of furniture in Quin's room.

The angel had a way of moving like liquid that was at once erotic and unsettling. It always left Quin feeling seasick.

Murmuration crossed to the bed and perched beside him. He trailed a hand over Quin's chest, over his belly, but no lower, only making the queasy feeling worse and leaving gooseflesh in his wake.

"Delicious, as always." A smile with too many teeth; a predator's smile.

Quin pushed himself to a sitting position, but he didn't quite have the strength to push Murmuration's hand away. The angel looked entirely too self-satisfied. The motion of his fingers gave the impression not just of touching Quin, but of sinking into him, seeking within him and pulling the choicest bits out to eat.

He knew if he searched his memory, last night would only come back to him in flashes, a series of still photographs with pieces missing in between. He remembered meeting Rowan. He remembered going to the second club. He'd found Murmuration there. He'd asked him for help with something – the case presumably – but why?

A dead pope, the kind of man who by default had too many enemies. Scribe IV had said there were no wounds on the body, no obvious cause of death. The only witness was a traumatized boy. It wouldn't be an easy case, but it wasn't impossible. Quin had barely tried, barely scratched the surface before running to his angel for help.

It had never been about the case, only his stupid weakness. Fuck. Lena would kill him when she found out. And somehow, she always did.

As if plucking thoughts from Quin's mind – and maybe that was precisely what he'd done – Murmuration stood.

"Don't worry your pretty head. I'll find the information you need. If I'm feeling kind, I'll even let you think it was your own brilliant detective skills that cracked the case." He leaned over, a looming shadow, cupping one hand behind Quin's head and touching the barest impression of a kiss to the corner of his mouth.

When he stepped back, the shiver that had been working its way to the surface since he'd woken rippled across Quin's body. He had too many questions; he couldn't pick just one. He put a hand to his head against a dull, building pain. What exactly had he asked the angel? What had he offered in return? A small piece of his soul? Nothing vital, surely. Nothing he would miss. The hell of it was, he'd never know.

Murmuration's expression settled into amusement – the amusement of the infinitely old faced with the infinitely young; indulgent patience. Irritation crept in, Quin's cheeks growing hot, his shoulders hunching in defense. The angel's expression didn't shift – or maybe it did, darkening, sharpening, gaining new edges.

"You're upset with me. You think I manipulated you into asking for my help so I could snap up more of your pretty, pretty memories." Murmuration brushed away Quin's objection with a long-fingered hand. "I'm not reading your mind, I'm reading your face. I'm offended, but don't worry, I'll still do the work and I'll find you when it's done."

In the angel's mouth, the words sounded almost like a threat. The accusations died, curling back into Quin's throat like a cut vine withering in the sun. He wanted to shout at the angel, demand he leave. Demand he return what Quin had lost, which he couldn't even remember. He wanted to hate someone else for his own weakness, and as always, Murmuration found a way to make that impossible.

The door slid open. Quin already felt a new kind of regret, the cold absence left in Murmuration's wake before he was even gone. But he had too much pride to call the angel back. To beg him to curl his terrible body around Quin's and hold him. He clamped his mouth shut.

Murmuration stepped over the threshold, accompanied by the faint sound of rustling wings. At some point, the door must have shut, but Quin missed it and by then, his angel was already long gone.

10

Scribe IV didn't experience any of the dizziness or nausea that Quin St. John seemed to when he was pulled through space, snapped from one location to the other by Angel. It was disorienting though, to be one moment in the tower and the next outside the Bastion's walls, standing near the ruins of the labyrinth. It left a faint ringing in his ears. Angel, however, looked delighted.

Xyr appearance had changed again, skin like basalt rock, cracked with veins of lava. When xe turned to grin at Scribe IV, xyr eyes were gold. Tiny flames danced among the strands of xyr hair. Xe wore an oversized beige trench coat, and xyr feet were bare despite the rough surface underfoot.

They stepped into the labyrinth together. Scribe IV recalled the last time the gardens and the labyrinth had been used for their original purpose, the rising chant as lines of novices and initiates, monks and nuns and priests wound their way through the twisting paths, censers and flickering beeswax candles in hand, the weight of ritual in the air. Once upon a time, they had elevated saints and made gods in this labyrinth. They had bound demons here, too, devoured their flesh and called it holy.

Two of the three moons had set while he and Angel were speaking in his tower. As on Heaven's Ark, traditional cycles of day and night didn't fully apply; the Bastion rarely saw actual sunlight. Not to mention that Scribe IV himself had no need of sleep. He hoped that Dominic had managed to rest at least, and Quin as well.

With the moons settling, the sky lightened, something approaching dawn, with the faintest blush of pale green behind a layer of clouds. Even abandoned, there was still a wild kind of beauty to the place. Porous stones rose like worn teeth, the ways between them winding arcane symbols over the landscape. Salt-eaten and wind-scoured, he could still see some of the original designs etched and painted on the stone.

Lichen grew on the rocks; other patches were spattered white with bird shit. Here and there, tiny star-shaped flowers with white and yellow petals pushed up through the stone.

Scribe IV stopped at the edge of what had once been the Chalice, in the deepest part of the labyrinth. Now it looked like a half-collapsed pit chewed into the stone. The clever system of pipes that had once fed it water from the sea had long been left to crumble, leaving it empty and dry.

Wind sighed over the stone, the pocks in the surface deep enough in some places to make a mournful sound – air across a dozen open mouths. The flames of Angel's hair shivered. Scribe IV turned, surveying the stone around them, looking for anything out of place.

"I contemplated the priesthood once," Scribe IV said.

He wasn't sure what made him say it, only that he'd been turning Angel's questions over in his mind. *Why did you come here? Why did you stay? If you weren't this, what would you be?*

"What stopped you?" Angel asked.

"The age-old debate over the nature and existence of the soul." It sounded strange, saying it aloud. Even admitting there was a controversy – or heresy, some would say – felt like giving it weight. Acknowledgment wasn't the same as belief, wasn't the same as aligning himself with one doctrine or another, but still. The fact that he couldn't dismiss the arguments that his mere existence was blasphemous, the fact that he'd ultimately chosen not to enter the priesthood, sometimes made him feel like a traitor to his own kind.

"Do you know that when the Scribe models were first introduced there was a call to destroy us? At worst, we were demonic – at best, an advanced form of mimeograph machine. How could we fail to taint the prayers of the faithful with our hands? We could copy them with great precision, translate and archive them flawlessly, tirelessly, but could we *understand* the nature of a prayer? How could a being without a soul be even a small part of the vast machinery of the church that stands between common humanity and Heaven, without bringing the whole of said machinery crashing down?"

"Humans are absurd," Angel said, an unshakable pronouncement of truth, which drew a startled sound from Scribe IV that might almost be categorized as a laugh.

"Yes, I suppose they are." He shook his head. "But still, even with the ratification by the Council of Erebus – and even though I would have been far from the first constructed being to take the sacred vows – I decided I didn't want to live with that doubt."

"Yours, or other people's?" Angel asked.

He opened his mouth to respond, but the words went unsaid, forgotten. Scribe IV bent to look at the white droplets spattering the rocks at his feet – beads of candlewax, not bird shit.

He crouched, and Angel crouched beside him, touching a finger to one of the drops.

"Look." A note of excitement crept into Angel's voice as xe pointed. "The dirt here is disturbed, like it's been swept around deliberately to hide footprints. Maybe someone camped here and left in a hurry. They could have left something else behind."

Xe stood, winding xyr way toward the other side of the labyrinth, and Scribe IV followed.

"If someone did camp here, they could have used the tunnels under the Bastion to get inside," Scribe IV said. It was only open ground between the labyrinth and Bastion otherwise, all visible from multiple points, including his own tower. "Part of the system connects to the pipes that used to feed the Chalice. Even if that is the case though, they probably would have needed help from inside. Sections of the tunnels are collapsed and to the best of my knowledge, there's no official map showing which are safe."

"Who among the staff would know the tunnels well?" Angel asked.

"Dominic," Scribe IV answered. "Agnetta too – she's the Chambermaid. And the Chatelaine." Scribe IV paused, feeling a flicker of guilt. "She claims not to like going down there. The Head Butler, as well."

"Would any of those people have a specific motive, a way they would be directly threatened or impacted by the conclave?" Angel asked.

"I... don't know."

He tried to think beyond his own biases, tried to recall what he knew of his staff beyond their work at the Bastion. Marius had a brother in the clergy; that might provide a motive of sorts. Dominic had said Johanna didn't like the Pope, but did he know that for a fact, or was it conjecture? Dominic liked to gather gossip, anything to relieve the boredom of days at the Bastion where nothing ever changed. He might have overheard something in the days leading up to the conclave.

It struck Scribe IV again that he'd asked the wrong questions of the boy, that he shouldn't have been the one to question him at all. He didn't want to believe any of the Bastion staff could be capable of murder, even those he didn't care for, who didn't care for him. But desperation could drive people to do terrible things. And faith could, as well.

"What's that?" Angel pointed, pulling Scribe IV away

from his grim thought. "That looks like something that could have been left behind, maybe."

Scribe IV looked to see something half-flattened that had been wedged into a gap in the stone. Hidden, dropped or accidentally kicked into place. He bent to pry it out, holding it up in the weird green light for Angel to see.

A metallic cylinder, not much longer than the space between the heel of his palm and the tip of his middle finger, cracked, perhaps where a careless boot had stepped on it.

Or where someone had tried to destroy evidence and, in their haste, done a poor job.

A faint tracery of numbers and letters remained visible upon its shattered side. "It looks like a container," Scribe IV said. "And this looks like a serial number, or at least part of one."

"It could be a clue." Enthusiasm had returned to Angel's voice, but Scribe IV couldn't shake a feeling of dread.

"Or it could be from the supplies delivered for the conclave," he said.

"What would it be doing near the labyrinth, then?" Angel asked. "Call it another hunch, but it seems out of place. If we can trace the serial number, maybe we can confirm what used to be in the container, and where it came from."

Xe grinned, spirit undampened. The wind picked up as they stepped around the last curve of the labyrinth and out onto the open cliffside again. It made Angel's hair crackle, whipping flames briefly into a streaming banner.

A figure stood between them and the path back to the Bastion. A figure that startled, before drawing herself up. Scribe IV recognized the silhouette – the Mother Superior. From her reaction, she hadn't come looking for them specifically. Searching for clues of her own then, or – the grim thought struck him – come to inspect the Chalice, to prepare it for a Drowning.

With a quick motion of his fingers, Scribe IV wedged the broken tube between the metallic bones of his forearm, dropping his sleeve to cover it and hoping she was too far away to see. He tried not to stand in a way that conveyed tension as the Sister approached.

"You are aware there is a curfew in effect?" the Mother Superior said.

"Yes." Scribe IV shifted closer to Angel. Xe had promised to protect him, but that didn't stop the fear clinging to his skin, sure as the salt-laden breeze. "I lost track of time. Apologies, Sister."

A blatant lie. His construction made it impossible to do something so human as to lose track of time, as he was certain the Mother Superior was well aware. The shape of her jaw was such that the Mother Superior couldn't press her lips into a thin line, nor hum her disapproval, but he felt it radiating from her nonetheless.

Scribe IV imagined another waterspout, called from the waves. He could almost hear the sound his bones would make, torn apart, the hidden cylinder revealed. He didn't have lungs, couldn't technically Drown, but he didn't doubt the Sisters' capacity for ingenuity in their cruelty.

The Mother Superior's gaze was fixed on him. Scribe IV held himself still. The singularity of her focus was unsettling, but the longer it went on, the more certain Scribe IV became that she wasn't waiting for him to crack. She was trying not to see Angel.

It was easy to ignore certain realities of divinity, to put forth your own interpretations of right and wrong, when your own god had been sleeping for countless years. It was much harder to ignore those realities when an angel was staring you right in the face.

Scribe IV met the Sister's eyes with somewhat less trepidation than he had a moment before.

"Is there anything else I might do for you, Sister? Were you in need of something, to be out here in the rising weather?"

The Mother Superior glared at him, or tried, but she couldn't quite hide her discomfort.

"You are aware that the Bastion is under the Sisterhood's full control, and that anyone failing to report even the most seemingly insignificant detail would, by their act of omission, be considered an accessory to the crime?" she said.

Her gaze, imperious and steady, didn't have the effect she intended. Not anymore. Scribe IV found himself amused. He could see even more clearly now how uncomfortable the Sister was. Angel made her nervous, and her threat fell flat.

"I am aware, Sister." He kept his tone neutral. "And I apologize for our violation of your curfew, but as neither of us are human and neither of us sleep, I thought it might be permissible to pass the time by showing my guest the grounds."

Scribe IV saw the Mother Superior flinch as he drew her attention to Angel's presence.

Beside him, Angel stretched. It was the only word Scribe IV could think to describe what he felt. Xe didn't move physically, but Angel expanded, as though part of xem now existed in the rocky ground on which they stood, in the air around them, perhaps even in the sea below the cliffs.

And if he could feel it, surely the Mother Superior could feel it too.

"Don't worry," Angel said, placing xemself directly in the Mother Superior's eyeline. "I'll see us both back inside safely."

The sweet innocence with which xe said it was belied by the tension Scribe IV felt where xyr hand rested on his shoulder. A subtle vibration, the effort of holding xemself back. The Mother Superior blanched. Her religious practice might not include angels, but she understood what angels were, what they could do. Her belief was not required. Angels were, and had always been, terrible things.

Angel's fingers curled subtly, whisking xemself and Scribe IV back inside the Bastion, letting their presence linger just long enough to see fear written clearly on the Mother Superior's face. It was immensely satisfying.

11

Lena stalked the corridors of Heaven's Ark, deck plates ringing under her feet. At least, she imagined they did – imagined, in fact, the entire structure of the station trembling beneath her wrath. Her fingers clenched at her sides, keeping the anger close. It was a useful thing. It was the only thing that would allow her to face down the angel while keeping the instinct to quake in his presence at bay.

Legion. Starling. Whatever the fuck the angel was calling himself these days. Quin had sworn he was done with the creature. But somehow, the angel had lured her brother back. And why wouldn't he? Lena generally found the proverb, which she always mentally translated as "scorpions will scorp," to be true. They would lash out to sting whether it was in their best interests or not. And when her dumbass brother was willing to serve himself up on a platter for the angel to pick his bones clean, why would that holy lamprey, freaky-ass vampire motherfucker turn down the chance?

After she was done screaming at the angel, she was going to kick Quin's ass.

The door waiting for her further down the corridor was a courtesy for the fragility of the human mind, acting as a threshold to a place that didn't truly exist on the station, or at least not solely on the station – everywhere and nowhere at once. It was the same door she had dragged Quin from nearly three years ago, when she'd placed him under her version of house arrest and made him quit both pixie dust and Starling in one go by denying him both.

The dust and the angel had been tearing Quin apart. She couldn't tell which was worse. Hollow – that was the best word she could think of to describe her brother in those days. Like the angel had reached right inside his skin and scooped out something fundamental. From what she understood, that was more or less what Starling had done. And Quin had all but begged to be scraped clean again and again. How thin could a bone be scraped before it snapped?

It was a question Lena clung to, telling herself she'd done it all for Quin's own good. Ignoring the tiny, vicious part of herself that wondered if she simply resented Quin for finding a way to forget, making her carry the memories alone.

All her anger had to be justified. Her brother must be in a bad way for Rowan to call her, practically sobbing, to admit he'd fucked up, had accidentally mentioned Starling's name. He'd sworn he hadn't meant to, that he'd been certain Quin already knew, apologizing to her over and over again. Lena didn't trust that motherfucker as far as she could throw him, and Rowan knew as much. So for him to reach out to her...

Lena stopped without intending to. She'd pictured striding straight up to Starling's door and smashing it with her fist, not letting her anger abate until she'd unleashed her tirade. Her breath slackened and her heartbeat slowed. The anger that had driven her here drained, leaving not fear, but something more like melancholy in its wake.

"Damn it." She paused, hand raised over the door-not-a-door.

The dizzying sensation of what lay on the other side reached for her – a void of white space so searingly bright it hurt her eyes just thinking about it.

(But if she had foregone knocking and strode through the door, letting go of the idea that it existed and embracing the knowledge that, contrary to her senses, nothing stopped her from simply stepping through to the place where the angel waited – she might have seen Starling curled small upon himself in the middle of the void. Floating upon the formlessness with his wings pulled tight about him, skin almost bleached of color, bones pressed out in knobs against that skin. She might have seen him shatter, becoming a murmuration in truth, swooping through that void and screaming against it. She might have seen him break apart and re-form over and over again, a keening, endless loop. And she might have known it for grief. But she did not. So the angel's sorrow unfolded with no witness at all, a lifetime in the space of a breath, in the time it took Lena's hand to approach the door-not-a-door as she at last gathered the courage to knock.)

She heard a whisper of sound in place of the storm she'd imagined, and the door slid open.

"Magdalena. Come in." She had the impression the angel was leaning on something, though there was nothing there to lean upon.

Starling looked haggard, a thing she hadn't known an angel could be. As she crossed the threshold, the blinding white of the angel's space rearranged itself to be friendlier to her eyes – something like an old-fashioned sitting room, wood glowing with a reddish hue, small end tables and brass lamps, overlapping carpets in jewel tones, floor-to-ceiling shelves and two wing-backed chairs.

She let go of her anger for long enough to sit, taking the cup the angel handed her. It was so fine as to be almost translucent, the same shade exactly as the long-fingered hand that passed it to her.

"Tea?" Starling asked as he took the chair opposite.

"Yes."

It struck Lena that she wasn't accepting, but agreeing, since he'd already handed her the cup before he asked. Between them, she and the angel were defining the nature of what was in the cup. *Yes, this is indeed tea that you have handed me*. If she'd said something else – brandy, or milk, or light wrung from a distant star – it would have been that, instead.

Stop it. Stop fucking with my head. She wanted to say it aloud, just like she wanted to call back her anger with him, the fury she'd felt stalking the corridors. But she said nothing. What was wrong with her?

"You're here about your brother," Starling said. Again, Lena felt his exhaustion, not an angel in this moment, but a hollow-boned bird in need of protection. "You're afraid for him, but I promise you there's no harm that wasn't already there long before I knew him, and I didn't do anything he didn't ask me to do."

Where she expected a smirk, a smooth, oily expression of contempt, she found only the shadow of a smile with nothing like joy in it. Another acknowledgment between them, but this time of everything broken in Quin. No matter what they did – no matter the violence with which they both might love him, in their own way – there was nothing either of them could do to fix it.

Lena was afraid for her brother; the angel was afraid for him too.

But that couldn't be right, could it? Angels didn't love humans.

Lena set her teacup down untouched.

"Where is he?" she asked.

"In his room. Sleeping. You could go talk to him." Starling's shoulders curled, not under the weight of wings, but in a gesture of something like defeat. His tone held the faintest note of reproach – like he was in a position to chide her for coming here, rather than going straight to Quin. Like she was hiding behind anger as an excuse to avoid the more painful thing that might be waiting for her.

Fuck, she hated him. Lena found words pouring out that she hadn't intended to say – not to the angel, not to anyone, not out loud at all, ever again. "When we were little, our father tried to make a god in the chapel behind our house—"

Starling held up a hand. "I know. I have eaten the memory a dozen times, or more."

Without moving, the angel suddenly stood over her, cupping her jaw and tilting her face upward. The impression filled her that there were words behind the ones the angel spoke aloud, an offer in the sorrowful expression in his eyes, spoken directly into her mind. *I could take this from you as well.* Lena's breath and heartbeat stuttered, and in that space, she almost missed the words Starling actually said.

"I know, Magdalena, because I have been there in the chapel with you every time the memory is devoured. I have felt it all as Quin felt it, and taken that from him. And I am sorry. Some wounds run too deep to heal."

Starling looked at her from the chair opposite hers, seated as though he'd never moved.

"Go talk to your brother."

The angel covered his eyes – the image of some classical sculpture from ancient history, half-remembered. His posture dismissed her without seeming to dismiss her. Lena moved to the door that wasn't a door.

"I will." Not because the angel told her to, because she wanted to, because it was the right thing to do. "Fuck you."

But she whispered it, and then not until she was back in the corridor outside the angel's room.

She tried to take comfort in the fact that he would hear her anyway, if he chose. It didn't make her feel any better at all. She steeled herself to go and talk to Quin.

~

She found her brother not sleeping, but at the tiny desk built into the room's wall, a plethora of screens spread across the surface before him.

"I'm looking at the temporary staff," Quin said without raising his head, as if he'd been expecting her, as if they were in the middle of a conversation. As if she hadn't had to travel all the way to Heaven's Ark at Rowan's plea, certain she would have to save Quin all over again. "Scribe IV gave me a full list. I figured someone's got to have a suspect past employment history, falsified references. But so far, everything checks out, they all have a clear pedigree. Not that it means any of them are innocent, but still, I was hoping for a place to start. As for the permanent staff, most of them were practically born into service, including a few literally left in the Bastion's care as babies, which doesn't really help me either. There's got to be something I'm missing. I just have to keep digging."

Quin still hadn't looked up during the torrent of words. Lena recognized it, the manic upswing. Starling had hollowed him out, leaving him clean and empty and fired with energy.

"Quin." Her eyes prickled.

"Lennie?" He raised his head at last, expression falling as he finally registered her. "What is it?"

He didn't remember. Of course he didn't. That was the whole point of feeding their fucking nightmare childhood to the angel. He'd gone and done it again. He'd left her alone.

"I—" Her voice broke.

Quin was up then, folding her in his arms. It was like being a child again, crossing the dark gulf between their narrow twin beds to tell him she'd had a bad dream. She sobbed against him, all the accusations she'd been ready to level dying on her tongue. For just a moment, she let herself fall apart. Let herself be the younger sibling and have Quin comfort her after years of holding it together, being strong, being okay when he was not.

He helped her sit, handed her a glass of water. Lena sipped, trying to ignore the stale recycled taste of it. She smeared a palm across her cheeks and forced a smile, self-deprecating and laced with salt.

"I'm sorry," she said.

"Why?" Quin sat, elbows on his knees, leaning toward her as if ready to catch her.

"This wasn't how any of this was supposed to go."

"Did something happen?"

Yes. A long, long time ago. But you wouldn't remember, not now anyway.

The image of Starling rose in her mind. A sorrowful angel. One who claimed he'd devoured Quin's bad memories dozens, maybe even hundreds of times. Who'd offered to do the same for her. Would it be so bad?

She understood the temptation. Throw it all away, start clean.

But it wasn't the answer. Because Quin did remember, somewhere deep down, even when he didn't. Otherwise, why go back to the angel again and again?

She couldn't hate him – even when she did a little, in a shameful, secret place she didn't want to look at. But she wouldn't say anything, couldn't be the one to drag the memory back up into the light, not when the scar was so new, so temporary, just waiting to split open again.

"Are you happy?" she asked instead.

It wasn't the question she'd intended to ask. She wasn't even sure she wanted it answered. She already knew – twelve therapists over twice as many years. Neither of them would ever be purely happy, no matter how she worked towards acceptance, forgiveness, understanding – of herself, even of her father.

She should be better than this. She'd worked hard to build a life for herself. She'd met and married a woman she loved, she was a tenured professor at a good university, she wasn't a scared child anymore – except sometimes, Lena was certain she'd never left that chapel. She was still there, waiting for their father to change his mind. Waiting to be saved.

She tried something else instead, rephrasing the question. "When's the last time you remember being happy?"

There had to be something – a time before it had all broken apart, or sometime since when the hurt had receded just enough to let some measure of joy through.

"That's a big and complicated question."

She leaned into him and let out a breath. Quin put an arm around her.

She could hear the frown in his voice, imagined his mind skipping over the new hole in his memory as he tried to come up with an answer. "There was…" He paused, gathering himself. "I don't remember the woman who gave birth to me, I was so young when she died and our father remarried. I only remember our mom, and I have this memory of her wearing a blue dress with little white polka dots on it. It must have been right before you were born, because her stomach was huge. The wind kept blowing the dress against her legs, and the sunlight behind her made her hair shine. She told me to listen for you, and I put my ear against her stomach and convinced myself I could hear you dreaming."

He coughed, embarrassed and self-conscious.

"What was I dreaming?" Lena asked.

She didn't want the moment to end. She barely remembered her mother, and Quin had never wanted to talk about her before.

"I don't know. Something beautiful, I hope." He shifted slightly, and she lifted her head to look at him.

"Tell me more?"

Her question was dangerous; any conversation about their past always was. At any moment, the ground might open beneath them, swallow them both whole.

"She used to sing lullabies. Do you remember?" Quin asked.

"No," Lena said. "I wish I could."

"Memory isn't all it's cracked up to be. There are times when all I can remember is the end, when she ran into the field and—shit. I'm sorry."

His breathing was speeding up. Lena had pushed too far. And part of her recognized that she'd done it willfully, because she was so fucking tired of being left alone.

Except Quin hadn't left her alone. Not then. Not the day their mother died. Lena had been playing on the kitchen

A. C. WISE

floor in a square of sunshine. Quin had come inside, folded
her in his arms and held her so tight she could scarcely
breathe. He'd only been eight, so she must have been three
or four. Too young to know what was going on. He'd held
her, sheltered her as best he could.

Looking back now, Lena knew their mother had been
scared of their father. She hadn't known how to find her
way to a place where she could take her children and leave.
She'd taken the only road she could see at the time, the
one that let her out, and left Lena and Quin behind.

"I'm sorry. I—" Quin's voice broke.

Lena could see it through his eyes, the ragged hole
where his memories stopped. There was confusion in his
expression. The growing darkness of the four years they'd
been left alone in their father's care. Four years where his
mind slowly rotted, his delusions growing ever worse.
And at the end, the chapel.

Her youth had shielded her – at least somewhat – along
with time, and the imperfection of memory. Even without
the benefit of an angel, there were things Lena simply
didn't know – how long they had spent sealed in the chapel,
bound in a parody of worship, waiting for their father's
god to wake. She didn't know how they'd left the chapel
either, only that she'd been fevered, slipping between
waking and dreaming. She remembered Quin pressing
her face to his side, cracked lips whispering *Don't look,
Lennie, don't look*.

She'd obeyed, and so she would never know what it
was she wasn't supposed to see. As much as she wanted to
blame him, even hate him at times, Quin had tried his best

to protect her. Even if it felt like he was always running away from her now.

"This was a mistake." Lena stood so fast she almost fell.

Quin caught her hand, squeezed it hard. She stopped, her eyes stinging. She couldn't look at him. Part of her wanted to go back to the angel and scream at him for real this time. Another part wanted to throw herself on his mercy.

Take it, take it all. I don't want any of it anymore.

"Lennie." When she turned back toward the sound of her name, Quin looked lost.

He couldn't even remember what he'd tried to give up so many times. But it was there, a shadow in his eyes. And she couldn't leave him alone with that, no matter that he'd left her.

All she wanted was to take his pain away. Even though she was the younger sibling, even though she hurt too, she wanted to throw her arms around him and take it all.

Was it possible Starling looked at her brother and felt the same? She'd come here wanting to hate the angel. She still wanted to – but was Starling trying to be kind?

Being in the angel's mere presence wore Quin away to nothing, like prolonged exposure to lead paint, or radium, or the sun – anything bright and deadly and beautiful.

Love like that would be like having the attention of a star, would burn the beloved to ash. And a tiny part of Lena wondered if it might be worth it.

"Fuck." She squeezed Quin's hand the way he'd squeezed hers.

He winced, and that finally got her to smile.

"Let me buy you noodles?" The offer and half-smile were an apology, even if Quin still didn't know exactly what he was apologizing for. It would have to do.

"Sure." Lena pulled him toward the door before she changed her mind. "You can tell me about this case you're working on while we eat."

12

Quin rotated the image of the partially crushed cylinder Scribe IV and Angel had found in the ruins of the labyrinth. He'd traced the number tagged on it back to the Hephaestus mining operation below Ganymede Station, but that still didn't tell him how the tube had ended up in the ruins outside the Bastion, or what – if anything – it had to do with the dead Pope.

He didn't want to bring Scribe IV and Angel more questions, a fragment of information that might be meaningless. Which was stupid. He was making things harder by not sharing the information. But his professional pride was stung, and he wanted to go back to them with an answer ready to serve up on a silver platter.

It was even worse than that. Some small, stupid part of him was waiting on Murmuration. Quin wanted the angel to return with whatever information he'd been able to dig up, so Quin could justify giving away whatever part of himself he'd given to buy it.

Or he simply wanted the angel to return to him.

Weariness on its way to becoming a headache pressed outward from the space between his eyes. Quin killed the screen, leaning back in his chair.

He was missing something. Clearly. He felt he could almost trace a finger around its edges, a ragged hole where the information should be.

What was it the boy at the Bastion had said?

It wasn't like him to forget details of a case like this – not mid-investigation. Why hadn't he left himself a note?

A note. Scribe IV had found a scrap of paper with the body. Maybe someone had been blackmailing the Pope. Fuck. No, that wasn't it, because the paper had been blank. Scribe IV had told them that, and it had slipped Quin's mind.

Something the boy had said about—

Everything jittered sideways. Quin caught himself just before he fell.

Fuck.

He wanted – no, he needed – a drink.

He'd been so charged up, so full of energy before Lena arrived, carrying a storm in her eyes. Now, he felt heavy. They'd talked, like they hadn't in a long time, but he was sure she was holding more back. He wanted to help unburden her, take care of her the way a big brother should, but he had no idea how.

He should have focused on the good memories of their mother – the songs, the lullabies, the games of hide and seek, building forts out of pillows and blankets on the wide back porch and sheltering under them to listen to the rain. He could have filled those memories in for

Lena. Instead, he'd blundered right up to the edge of their mother's death.

He'd come dangerously, selfishly, carelessly close to telling her everything he remembered. But he couldn't taint the few memories Lena had of their mother. She shouldn't have to drag around the quilt of horrors he did, stitched to the good memories, always a few steps behind, waiting to trip him the moment he let his guard down.

A knife – serrated like the bones of a spine – gripped in his mother's hand. It must have been an ordinary breadknife; awful enough, but in his mind's eye, it had taken on demonic proportions. As long as her forearm, its teeth distinct blades in and of themselves. The plink, plink, plink of blood hitting the porch – though he couldn't have heard it, the blood didn't come until later. A storm on the horizon, the sky yellow like old bone, slate-gray clouds pressing in behind it. Their mother's hair all loose, her feet bare, looking back at him with shadowed eyes, before running into the field. Her shape flickering between the laundry flapping on the line.

The way he remembered it, no one had ever pulled that laundry down. With everything that came after, it had been left there and the storm had torn it to shreds. It was still there now in Quin's mind, tattered strips of gray, fluttering in the breeze.

She'd been afraid. And at the end, that fear had outweighed her love.

He might have run to her, run with her. Everything might have been different.

But Lena had called out from inside the house. He couldn't leave her. How could their mother?

He went back inside and sat with Lena while she played with her toys on the kitchen floor. And when their father finally returned, thunderously drunk, Quin had sent him back out into the field after their mother. He took his sister upstairs, made sure Lena brushed her teeth, tucked her into bed and read her favorite bedtime story. All the while, he'd been listening for the back door. For their father's footsteps on the stairs. Knowing what his father would find in the field. Waiting for the blame to fall on him.

The door chimed. Quin leapt to his feet, pulse thudding, and for a moment, he couldn't work out where he was, or when. He expected the farmhouse door. Expected a man in a hat and suit come to talk to his father about funeral arrangements. His father's refusal to bury his wife anywhere holy, because she was a suicide. Quin almost looked for Lena, to lead her away, shelter her, before his awareness of time and place resettled around him.

He palmed open the door.

Murmuration stood on the other side holding a single black rose. Since when did his angel knock? The rose's petals drank the light, giving it a faint shimmer that made Quin think of velvet and the darkness of space. It left him dizzy.

Quin accepted the flower, looking stupidly up from the fathomless petals to the angel's equally unsettling eyes.

"What?" Not the most elegant of greetings.

"I'm here to take you on a date." Murmuration's tone was formal; his smile did not touch his eyes.

"What?" Quin continued to stare, snagged by a tide, pulled under.

"A date," the angel said, patient, but Quin sensed an edge to it, the kind that cut straight to his spine, leaving his nerves raw and exposed.

"Or," the angel went on, "if you would prefer, a business meeting. If you still believe I manipulated you into giving me your memories." That edge again, tilted in a way Quin couldn't comprehend. He couldn't tell which direction it was meant to cut.

Murmuration held out his hand. Quin wanted very badly to take it, but felt he shouldn't. His knees were simultaneously locking him in place and turning to jelly. His fingers twitched at his side. *Guilt*. He'd never gotten a straight answer from Lena as to why she'd suddenly shown up at his door. If she knew he'd gone to see Murmuration, surely she would have cursed him out? The idea that she hadn't made him feel worse.

He still wanted to go with the angel.

Lena deserved better from her brother. But he didn't step back, say no, close the door.

"I promise I'll be a perfect gentleman. I won't lay a hand on you. Cross my heart." Murmuration held Quin's gaze. The angle of his lips spoke of cruelty, but his eyes said something else altogether.

Murmuration had told him once that angels had no soul, that their hearts were the only thing they could swear on.

Quin stepped forward, caught in the angel's magnetic pull. Feathers rustled, a sibilant music. His hand landed in the angel's – long fingers, cool and smooth like marble, closed around his, sending lightning through his veins.

He could resist, *should* resist, should slam the door in the angel's face, and absolutely no part of him wanted to. Murmuration slid an arm around his shoulders – possessive, protective – and led Quin down the corridor.

"What are we doing here?" Quin leaned closer to be heard over the music.

He kept his eyes fixed on the stage, where projected black and white circles spun in a pinwheel pattern. He'd never been to Cirque on a night when Rowan wasn't performing, and it felt weirdly like a betrayal.

"I'm delivering on a promise." Murmuration's voice, silk and cream, sounded much closer than it should, perfectly audible over the music that stole all other sound.

The angel draped one arm across the back of the booth, but carefully kept it from touching Quin. Even so, Quin felt the brush of lips at his ear with the angel's words and fought down a shudder.

"Hush now, and watch the show."

Confused, Quin obeyed. The light spun away and returned a moment later, illuminating two naked dancers on the small, circular stage. One's skin had been painted metallic silver, the other gold. The gold dancer's skin was covered with elaborate, intricate tattoos. But shouldn't the paint cover them? Quin tried to puzzle it out, but the music rose and the dancers clasped hands, swirling around each other. It took Quin a moment to realize the gold dancer's tattoos had shifted – not a simple pattern anymore, but words he wasn't quite close enough to read.

Quin's breath snagged. The words left the gold dancer's body altogether, like insects, like smoke, flowing onto the silver dancer's body, forming a twisting pattern of chains, interlocking spirals, galaxies unfurling.

Insects flowing—

No.

Crawling.

The crawling dark.

Flies stepping across his skin, speaking words he tried desperately not to hear.

Quin's stomach cramped, sweat prickling, jaw clenched. Something terrible. Something familiar. Something he needed to remember.

Murmuration's fingers tangled through his, squeezing hard, holding him in place and grounding him. The angel leaned close, his voice pitched to soothe, as if Quin were a skittish animal.

"Shhh. I have you. You're safe. Just watch. This is the information you paid me for, after all. Let me give it to you."

There was something almost mocking in the angel's voice. Almost cruel – but sorrowing as well.

Quin was falling – would fall – had already fallen – but Murmuration caught him.

A thread snapped, unwound.

Not the crawling dark – and where had that phrase come from?

Tattoos. Ink. But not *ink*.

Nanites, following their programming, pulsing in time with the music, dancing their own dance over the performers' skin. Nanites, which miners and mining bots carried in tubes like the one Scribe IV had found. Nanites, ready to be poured into jammed equipment too delicate for human hands or metal tools to fix. Nanites that could burrow away blockages, extract precious elements from stone, could even travel through the blood vessels inside a human being to prevent a cardiac arrest. Or cause one.

The blank piece of paper Scribe IV had found in the Pope's hand. What if it hadn't always been blank? What if someone had delivered a note to His Holiness, and the words had crawled – that word again, that fucking word, why did it grate at him every time he found it in his head?

Because the chapel—

No.

The ink had slipped right off the page and into the Pope's body, leaving His Holiness holding his own murder weapon. Dominic had tried to describe it, tried to tell them the only way he knew how.

What a child's mind could conjure in a moment of stark fear. A demon of swirling smoke, felling the Pope. A—

god—

Quin's head felt ready to split wide. He pushed away from the table, stumbling toward the door.

He'd put the pieces together. He should be pleased. Why did it all feel so fucking wrong?

Like he'd been falling for a very long time.

Into the—

—crawling dark, the only place to look was up, into the corner, the place he didn't want to look, because Quin had broken, he'd let fear strip everything away from him and in desperation, he'd prayed. More than prayed. In that moment, he'd believed

with every part of himself that the dark and terrible god above him was his only salvation, that it could save him. He'd given it his love. And when he had, his father's god had opened terrible eyes and spoken a holy word—

He crashed to his knees outside the club, hard decking jarring against bone, slamming his hands to either side of his head to keep it from breaking apart. He couldn't breathe, throat closing. Tears stung his eyes.

No.

Nonono.

The thread unwound, back, back, spooling all his memories in until—

Clean laundry fluttered in the breeze. His mother smiled at him. White polka dots against blue the same color as the sky, her hair blowing in the wind. She pulled him against the moon of her belly and whispered, "Listen."

He did, hearing his sister dream.

The thread snapped, gathered in long-fingered white hands.

Quin lifted his head.

He must have tripped on his way out of the club, though he didn't even remember getting up from the table to leave. He pushed himself upright. Murmuration had delivered on his promise, helped Quin connect the dots. He had to get to Scribe IV and Angel. He would thank the angel later. Or not.

Quin broke into a jog.

"You're welcome." Murmuration's voice trailed after him, a feather brushing against his ear and tracing along the length of his jaw.

13

"That blank piece of paper you found on the Pope's body," Quin said almost as soon as Angel materialized them in the tower room.

Scribe IV looked up from his desk, startled. It wasn't Quin's and Angel's appearance itself – that he had expected. Angel had received Quin's prayer, attuned and listening for him, and had gone to Heaven's Ark to fetch him. It was Quin's expression that caught Scribe IV off guard – not the queasy expression of being pulled through space, but a glassy, almost fevered look. As if he'd been running moments before he arrived. As if something had been chasing him.

Without being asked, Scribe IV poured a drink and passed it to Quin. He did not miss the tremor in the man's hand as he accepted it, or the look on his face, simultaneously distracted and grateful.

"The paper," Scribe IV said, prompting Quin.

"Right." Quin snapped his fingers, forcibly pulling himself together, but the shine hadn't left his eyes, nor had the sense of manic energy dispelled from around him.

He struck Scribe IV as someone waking from a dream – or more accurately, a nightmare – and desperately trying to recall what he'd seen. A man trying to recapture a word on the tip of his tongue, all the while afraid the word was barbed, that he would accidentally swallow it down.

"The paper. That's our murder weapon," Quin said. "The tube you found used to hold nanites, and they were trained to mimic ink, to spell words. The… thing Dominic saw in the room…"

Quin's expression slackened, some internal struggle Scribe IV couldn't guess at happening behind his eyes. Then he shook himself, and as if he'd never stopped, went on. "He saw nanites. They spelled out a message on that paper. Once the Pope read it, they poured themselves into his bloodstream, up his nose and into his airways – stopping his heart, stopping his breath, killing him in whatever way they were programmed to do, then fleeing the scene."

"How did you determine this?" Scribe IV asked.

"I…" Quin stopped himself, looked troubled. He sipped from his drink. It seemed to center him. "… went to a show that used nanites to mimic tattoos on the dancers' bodies. It gave me a flash of inspiration. I thought of that blank piece of paper in the Pope's hand, how it didn't make sense."

He grinned, but the expression looked strained to Scribe IV, fragile and painful.

"It's possible the nanites left a trace. We might be able to reconstruct the message, though I fear that would require time and specialized equipment we don't have." Scribe IV retrieved the paper and set it on his desk.

"I might be able to help," Angel said. "If you would like me to."

Xyr appearance had settled somewhere between xyr last two iterations – the slight, gamine frame with skin that at least nodded to the possibility of being human, while xyr hair rustled softly with flames. Xe wore a loose-knitted garment that fell past xyr knees. Angel played with the cuffs of its overly long sleeves as xe spoke. Xyr feet, still bare, made no noise as xe padded across the floor to Scribe IV's desk.

Xe glanced at him for permission – an uncertainty that again made Scribe IV think of Angel as young. Scribe IV inclined his head, but it occurred to him that Angel wanted, or needed, him to say the words aloud.

"Yes, please help reconstruct the message if you can."

It wasn't quite a prayer, but it was enough. Angel held xyr palm over the paper.

A small miracle, performing the work of the equipment they didn't have. A humming sensation crawled across Scribe IV's gleaming bones. The paper shimmered, words ghosting into view. Quin had drawn closer as well, but now he took a step back.

"Are you unwell?" Scribe IV asked. He held out his hands, ready to catch Quin, who for a moment looked faint.

"Something about…" Quin waved a hand, swallowed hard. "I don't know. The way they move. They make me seasick." He pulled over a chair and sat. "I'll be fine."

Scribe IV turned his attention back to the page, to the words, which had stilled now – an echo of ink that wasn't ink, made visible by Angel's grace. Faint signs of strain showed in Angel's expression. Scribe IV read the words aloud quickly so xe could let go.

> *Your family has spent generations bleeding Hephaestus dry. Your great-grandfather, your grandfather after him, but your father worst of all. He wasn't content with the mines. He exploited the people too, took what he wanted and left my mother pregnant with twins. He left us to starve. The money that bought your papacy should have been ours. We want what we're owed.*

Scribe IV exchanged a glance with Angel. Family. Scribe IV felt a twinge of recrimination. It should have occurred to him sooner. He should have considered the possibility of a motive that was more personal than the Pope's proposal to abolish established religion. After all, wasn't that the whole point? The Pope spoke for his god, but he was only human. Human, and just as capable of being brought down by jealousy, love, betrayal, greed, as anyone else.

"Shit. So the Pope's father knocked up someone on Hephaestus and left two kids behind. One of those kids turned up to blackmail him… No." Quin snapped his fingers again, stringing pieces together as Scribe IV watched. "No, because why use nanites to deliver a simple blackmail note? The intent was always murder, and blackmail was just a decoy – an excuse to deliver a note, and a message dramatic enough that the Pope would actually stop and read it. And maybe a way for the murderer to get some anger off their chest at the same time, telling the Pope exactly how they felt they'd been wronged."

"If the Pope already carried guilt over his family purchasing his title," Scribe IV said, "he would have wanted to set things right."

"Revenge is pretty solid, as motives go," Quin said. "Even if the killer went after the son, not the father. I mean, the Pope's father is already dead, so he made the next most convenient target. The conclave provided the perfect cover for the killer with all the temporary staff arriving and shuttles delivering supplies."

"It's still likely that whoever brought the nanites had help from inside," Scribe IV said. "Large sections of the tunnels are collapsed; they're almost impossible to navigate for those unfamiliar with them. A member of the Bastion staff would also be less suspect delivering the letter to the Pope's room. It could have been delivered with a meal."

Or with the tea service, which had still been sitting in the room with the Pope's corpse, waiting to return to the kitchen. Johanna and Marius had both been close enough to hear Anna-Maria scream when she'd seen the Pope's body, but none of them had been into the Pope's room to collect the tray.

Because Dominic had been in there first.

He'd told Scribe IV that's why he'd been in the room, and Scribe IV had believed him. But he'd released Dominic from his duties for the day when the boy came to deliver his report. So why would he be there? An answer came to him, but he didn't like it.

Dominic would have entered the room if he thought

he was covering for Agnetta, bringing back the tray she'd forgotten to return so she wouldn't get in trouble.

Agnetta wasn't one to shirk her duties or be forgetful. Why hadn't she returned for the tray? Perhaps she'd been afraid to go back into the room. But what motive could Agnetta possibly have?

There was something Scribe IV had forgotten. Something he'd deliberately put aside.

Scribe IV wanted to rest his head against the stone wall and let it take the weight of polished metal. He was a thing no machine should be: he was tired.

"You okay?" Quin touched Scribe IV's arm.

"I believe I know who within the Bastion may have a connection with Hephaestus, and thus a reason to help our murderer."

Scribe IV ran metallic fingertips down the side of the desk until he heard a faint *click*. Doing what he should have done long before now – or undoing what he never should have done in the first place.

He pulled out the long, thin drawer, just wide enough to hold a rack of gleaming capsules. The rack chimed faintly as he lifted it free.

"What are those?" Quin asked.

Scribe IV noted that while he looked at the capsules with interest, Quin didn't come any closer to the desk, and he carefully did not look at the paper that had recently held the ghostly imprint of the nanites.

"Memories," Scribe IV said.

Like everything else about him – the delicate work of his bones, his jeweled gears – these too were designed to be lovely as well as functional. Scribe IV hated looking at them. "These are ones that are… painful. I deliberately set them aside."

"You can do that?" Quin asked, a shadow that Scribe IV could not quite read crossing his features.

"A simple download to external storage. The memories no longer take up space in my primary core, but they are preserved should they ever be needed." He touched the three most recent capsules, dates etched along their sides. Altogether, there were too many of them. "Every child ever left at the Bastion is here."

Scribe IV let his fingertips pass over the entire row of capsules. As long as there had been humans, there had been stories of babies abandoned to the mercy – or wrath – of the gods. Children left on temple steps, at the doors of churches. Babies exposed on cliffsides, or cast down from them, left in the woods to the hunger of wolves. Some were lucky enough to be raised in faith and love by acolytes; some had their eyes bound and their lips sewn shut to better hear the whispers of dread gods. Others were killed outright, not by their parents, but by the supposed faithful charged with their care. He'd heard stories of infants bricked up inside the walls of holy places, and others fed into fires as a stand-in for the mouth of god for the sole sin of they themselves being one mouth too many to feed.

Scribe IV lifted the second capsule from the long row, tucked in between Dominic's, the most recent, and Justine, the child before him – save one.

Agnetta.

He felt Quin and Angel watching him. Scribe IV pushed back his sleeve, slotted the capsule into a port between his bones.

"Agnetta's mother surrendered her to the Bastion's care twenty-two years ago," he said.

The memory unfurled from the capsule's files. A dark-haired woman, features much like Agnetta's. She'd been younger than Agnetta was now, but looked older – harried and planed sharp by life. She held a bundle in her arms – not just one child, but two. Twins she could not afford to raise; she'd begged the Bastion to take them into its care.

"Agnetta and her brother," Scribe IV said.

Angel touched his arm in a comforting gesture, concern shining in xyr eyes.

"The Chatelaine at the time refused to take on more than one child. He told Agnetta's mother she would have to choose." Scribe IV placed his own hand next to Angel's, covering the capsule still fitted into his arm, as if he could contain the hurt there.

The way Agnetta's mother had howled, threatening to throw both children and herself from the cliffs. The Chatelaine plucking Agnetta from her arms, taking the choice from her. She hadn't thrown herself or the boy into the sea, but returned to the shuttle with hunched shoulders, baby pressed to her chest as if she could protect him from the rain that left them both soaked to the bone.

And Scribe IV had stood next to the Chatelaine and done nothing but watch. Complicit.

"Our numbers were at least twice what they are now, but only a fraction of what they had been at their height.

It would not have been so much of a burden to take both children, and their mother even, but the then-Chatelaine would not be moved. He refused, insisting that more than one child would be too much to manage."

Shame burned through him, another thing metal should not be able to feel. "I should have pleaded the mother's case. I should have at least tried."

Scribe IV lifted his hand from his arm, let it drop to his side, the gesture weighing his shoulders down. Now that he'd accessed the memory, he could not stop seeing the bruised look of Agnetta's mother's skin. She had been fleeing violence as well as starvation – he was certain of that now. If both mother and child had survived, he could only imagine what their life had been from that moment on.

Scribe IV had watched through the rain until the shuttle winked out in the sky over the Bastion – a falling star in reverse. Then he'd returned inside, and – in a final act of betrayal to Agnetta's mother and her pain – he'd put the memory aside.

The pressure of Angel's fingers on his arm increased. The sympathy in the touch was undeserved. He'd been selfish, hoping for acceptance among the human staff. He'd held his silence and gone along with what he knew to be wrong, hoping that if he didn't make trouble, if he sided with them, they might stop seeing him as a blasphemy.

"Life in the mining colonies is bad now, but it was even worse back then. I might as well have condemned Agnetta's mother and brother to death." Scribe IV made himself meet Angel's eyes.

Angel's gold-hued gaze held steady. There was compassion there, but xe didn't tell Scribe IV it wasn't his fault. Xe didn't offer forgiveness, knowing it would be refused. Xyr touch said only that Scribe IV wasn't alone in his pain, and for that, he was grateful.

"Agnetta's brother might have survived and still be living in the colony," Quin said. "It's a tenuous connection, but right now, it's all we've got."

"We need to find Agnetta," Scribe IV said.

He could have done more for the child Agnetta had been, for her mother, her brother. Where did that sense of duty – that guilt – leave him? If Agnetta had indeed been party to murder, or committed the murder herself, he could cover for her. He could try to help her escape. It wouldn't change the choice Scribe IV had made twenty-two years ago. It wouldn't undo her mother's and brother's suffering, or even Agnetta's own, growing up without her family.

It would also make him an accomplice to murder.

Scribe IV moved toward the door, Angel and Quin following. He didn't know what he would do when they found Agnetta – if they found her. Selfishly, all he wanted was to somehow be proven wrong.

14

He was so preoccupied with his thoughts that Scribe IV didn't see Dominic seated on the bottom step leading up to his tower until he nearly tripped over him. The boy jumped up, shoving something into his pocket as he did.

"Sir—" he began, but Scribe IV interrupted him, taking the boy's shoulders as gently as he could.

"Have you seen Agnetta?"

A host of emotions passed through Dominic's eyes, like a swift flock of birds.

"I…" Dominic looked down, chewed his lip along with whatever decision he had to make, then lifted his head to meet Scribe IV's gaze.

Tears glazed the boy's lower lids, but he kept his chin up and did not let them fall, his voice quivering only very slightly as he spoke.

"I was coming to find you, sir. Or…" He gestured at the steps, where he'd presumably been gathering his courage. "Agnetta said she had to go away, and not to tell. I'm scared something bad happened to her, because otherwise, why wouldn't she take me with her? She's always taken care of me, and… She gave me this."

Dominic dug in his pocket for the object he'd stowed there, holding it up in the corridor's dim light. A necklace, a small, pressed tin medallion spinning at the end of the chain. Scribe IV stilled the small oval long enough to see the image of the saint it bore – St. Jude, protector of children.

"She said it belonged to her mother a long time ago, and it would watch over me once she was—" Dominic's voice broke, losing his battle against tears.

"You did the right thing, Dominic." Scribe IV made his voice as soft as he could. "Do you know where Agnetta went? I'll help her if I can."

"The lower tunnels." Dominic scrubbed the back of his hand across his eyes and under his nose. "It's the best place for hide and seek."

"I'll make sure she's safe," Scribe IV said. He pressed the medallion into Dominic's hand. "I promise. In the meantime, you hold onto this for her."

"Can I help you look for her?" The hope in the boy's eyes pained Scribe IV. He shook his head.

"Go to the kitchen and wait with Seb. You'll be safe there."

Scribe IV glanced at Angel and Quin, who'd watched the exchange silently. Dominic looked between the three of them, clearly hoping Scribe IV would change his mind. When he did not, the boy turned, dragging his steps, stalling and glancing back over his shoulder.

It was cruel, making a promise Scribe IV wasn't sure he could keep.

"Can you hold a picture of the tunnels in your mind?" Angel asked once Dominic was no longer in sight. Xe held out xyr hand, voice soft. "I can take us straight there."

"Yes." Scribe IV didn't know exactly where Agnetta might be, but he could picture the ruined maze, the storage areas where moth-eaten tapestries and worn statues lay in repose, eventually giving way to the crypts and then to caves above the sea.

The tunnels might have shifted since he'd last been down there, new sections collapsing and closing off passages. All he could do was hope that Angel wouldn't materialize in the midst of a spill of rock, or in a sinkhole dropping straight into the sea.

Scribe IV placed his hand in Angel's. Xe held out xyr other hand for Quin. Space folded around them. Scribe IV was grateful he did not have breath to lose. It was different, being pulled through the Bastion, rather than transported outside of it. He could not quite shed his awareness of the layers of stone, and was grateful when they came to rest in the warren of tunnels on solid ground.

"This is where..." Quin put out a hand to steady himself against the rough stone. "The boy, last time I was here."

Scribe IV knew he meant the boy who had become a god in the caves above the sea. Perhaps it was the fact of being underground, or letting Angel transport him twice in quick succession, but Quin looked downright haunted.

Scribe IV produced a light, holding it up so shadows dragged along the walls in its wake. He hadn't been sure where to direct Angel. Agnetta would likely choose somewhere remote, one of the lowest, oldest tunnels, especially if her eventual goal was to descend the cliffs to the sea in hopes of making an escape.

The space felt wilder, more abandoned than the last time he'd been here. The sea felt closer as well, a fist pounding on the walls and demanding entrance. At least he could use the sound to orient himself, and he turned them toward the cliffs and the caves.

The stone was uneven, and Scribe IV moved slowly, Quin and Angel following. There were any number of side tunnels, alcoves, half-fallen passageways where Agnetta might hide herself. He didn't want to miss one, but he was sharply aware that they were running out of time. They might already be too late.

"You're doing everything you can." Angel's voice reached him, accompanied by a spreading glow, allowing Scribe IV to see the way ahead more clearly.

He glanced back. Angel's skin shone luminous, xyr smile quietly encouraging.

Scribe IV appreciated what xe was trying to do, though it shouldn't have been necessary. Machines didn't feel fear. They didn't feel sympathy for murderers. They didn't put aside memories they found inconvenient. He might not be a blasphemy, but he had grown beyond the original intent of his programming. He had lived too long and had become, in his own way, a sinner.

The ground sloped gently but steadily downward. The walls pressed in, the way narrower, the ceiling lower, forcing Scribe IV to stoop so he was almost bent double.

The back of his robe scraped against rock as he squeezed under an arch of stone that let out into an open space he didn't recognize. Several walls had collapsed, opening up the formerly honeycombed space of chambers and winding paths into something that almost looked like an underground forest. Or a cathedral. Odd pillars of stone, whittled almost to nothing by the wind and water, growing up from the floor like petrified trees.

Pale green-gray light filtered through the stone forest. At the far end of the cave, the wall had worn away entirely, opening out onto the sea. The waves reached high enough that Scribe IV could see the spray where they smashed against the rock.

Above the boom of the surf, he caught the sound of stone sliding against stone. Quin turned at the same moment Scribe IV did.

His light pinned Agnetta as she caught herself against one of the pillars of stone, loose rocks sliding beneath her feet. She threw an arm up to shield her eyes, dazzled. She was soaked to the bone, uniform clinging to her body, hair trailing in wet tendrils around her face. She must have been looking for a way down and, failing to find one, turned back to try again.

"Agnetta." Scribe IV took a step forward, hands outstretched in what he hoped was a reassuring gesture as he spoke.

"Don't," Agnetta said. Her outstretched hands mirrored his, her voice sharp.

Scribe IV reeled back just in time, understanding her words for a warning. Just beyond the pile of fallen rock he'd been about to step over, the floor had collapsed. Water had flooded the cave below, surging in with the tide. If he'd taken that step, he would have fallen and been swept out to sea.

"We want to help you." Scribe IV pitched his voice to be heard over the roar of the tide. "I should have helped you sooner."

Agnetta trembled – whether from cold, from being soaked to the bone, or from anger or fear, Scribe IV couldn't say.

"I know your mother and brother must have both suffered terribly, and I'm sorry," he said. "I'll do what I can to help—"

"My mother is dead." Agnetta cut across Scribe IV's words, her voice bitter. Her expression fell, her voice growing quieter, but not so quiet that he couldn't pick it up over the rush of the tide. "At least that's what my brother told me. He found me here, told me how he'd watched her die, how lucky I was, how miserable their lives had been. He said I owed him my help. I wanted to help." Agnetta's voice shook, a sound on the verge of tears. "He was in so much pain. He said he'd wait, we'd leave together once we had the money. We could take Dominic with us, and I could give them the life we never... I don't know if he meant any of it, I don't even know if he knew himself. I don't think my brother was well, but I thought if I could... I didn't know. I didn't know it was more than a blackmail note. I—"

Her voice broke. She covered her face with her hands, shoulders hitching. Scribe IV calculated where he might step across to reach her. The floor was riddled with holes, fragile, but she had crossed it so there must be a way.

"Forget it," Quin said. By his expression, he'd had the same idea as Scribe IV. "Your frame is too heavy. No offense. But the ground won't hold you."

As he spoke, Quin moved. Rock shifted dangerously, a slide like the one Agnetta had started. Quin improbably maintained his balance and took another step.

"You can't guarantee it will hold your weight either," Scribe IV said. "It's too dangerous."

Quin didn't stop moving, picking his way slowly across the floor. Agnetta hadn't lowered her hands from her face. She hadn't tried to move away either, possibly not hearing Quin's approach or their words over the crashing tide. Scribe IV, however, heard Quin perfectly when he spoke again, along with the grim determination in his voice.

"Lucky I'm an idiot with no sense of self-preservation, then."

Even as he spoke, he slid again, just managing to catch himself before he fell.

"Can you—" Scribe IV turned toward Angel; not a prayer, but a question.

If xe couldn't transport Agnetta without her consent, xe could at least transport xemself to her. Angel's expression kept the rest of Scribe IV's question unasked. Xe stood very still, xyr already pale skin even whiter somehow. Xe trembled, not the way Agnetta did, not with cold or fear, but with what Scribe IV could only think was restraint. A coiled spring, waiting to be released, holding xemself forcibly back from… something.

Angel's eyes had taken on the aspect of smoked glass, cracked, looking somewhere far beyond the cave. If xe had been human, Scribe IV would have said xyr eyes were rolled back in xyr head, like someone dreaming.

Scribe IV could almost feel it, though he couldn't describe it. A sound that wasn't a sound, like the tolling of the Sisters' bell, but deeper. A voice, calling, words that crawled across Scribe IV's skin but that he couldn't hear, because they weren't meant for him.

"Angel." He made to reach for xem. At the same time, Quin spoke from across the cave, drawing Scribe IV's attention.

"Agnetta."

Agnetta dropped her hands at the sound of her name. Quin reached for her. She batted his hand away, tried to move away. Her heel caught, tipping her too far backward. Quin lunged as her arms pinwheeled. The motion overbalanced him as well, and Agnetta was already falling. Their combined weight was too much. The rock gave, and Quin and Agnetta dropped out of sight.

A shout of alarm, a warning too late, locked in Scribe IV's throat. He whipped around to Angel, to pray if needed. Angel's trembling had grown worse. Xyr eyes were no longer smoked glass, but a color Scribe IV couldn't name. Xyr expression was of stark fear and sorrow, all wrapped in one.

"I'm sorry," Angel said.

Shame washed xyr features. Scribe IV stared at Angel, uncomprehending.

"We have to—" He made a move toward where Agnetta

and Quin had fallen, but Angel caught his arm in a violent grip.

"You can't," Angel almost shouted the words, voice rising dangerously close to a wail. "Only I can…"

Xyr expression crumbled, fingers digging harder into Scribe IV's arm. Wisps of smoke rose from beneath Angel's fingers. Scribe IV pulled back, and Angel let go.

"Why wouldn't they pray?"

Quin knew what Angel could do, knew xe could save him.

But Scribe IV knew the answer. It crouched in his mind, an ugly thing he couldn't deny. The pain in Agnetta's eyes. The shadow that had been haunting Quin since he'd arrived in Scribe IV's tower. Neither Quin nor Agnetta had wanted to be saved. In their hearts, neither believed salvation was possible for them, or that they were deserving of an angel's grace.

"We have to get down to where the cavern washes out," Scribe IV said.

He didn't want to contemplate what might be waiting for them. He should have acted. He should have at least tried. He shouldn't have put his memories aside in the first place.

Angel placed xyr hand on his shoulder, gently this time. No smoke rose, but the fabric of Scribe IV's sleeve was singed from xyr earlier touch. There was a *whump* of displaced air and Scribe IV was pulled inside himself, reappearing with Angel's hand still on his shoulder on the rocky shore. The tide boomed, salt spray filling the air and settling on his metallic skin.

They were too late. Again.

The leviathan slithered forward, water sluicing from its riveted skin. Two coiled limbs burst free of the waves, each holding a dripping form. Quin and Agnetta. Scribe IV couldn't tell if they were alive.

Spotlight-eyes bloomed on the ship-creature's surface, silhouetting Agnetta and Quin. A foghorn voice tolled the Drowned Sisters' proclamation loud enough to be heard over the surf.

"Aquinas St. John. You have been found guilty of interfering in a murder investigation and thus abetted and aided in the perpetrator's escape from justice."

The limb holding Agnetta twitched, as if to illustrate the voice's point. The light beaming from the leviathan showed Agnetta's bare feet. She'd lost her shoes. Scribe IV registered the angle of her neck. Dead – either in the fall or in the churning waves.

But the Sisters, whatever else they might be, were not frivolous. They had not addressed Agnetta, merely recovered her corpse. They wouldn't bother pronouncing sentence on a dead man. Quin confirmed as much with a feeble kick, but the limb wrapped around him held tight.

In the next moment, Scribe IV's hope dropped out completely.

"For these crimes, Aquinas St. John," the Sisters intoned, "you will be Drowned."

15

"What do we do?" Scribe IV had never felt more like a coward.

Angel hadn't spoken since pulling them back up to the caverns, to a niche where they had a view of the beach but were safe from the water, where the floor was stable enough that they wouldn't fall. Below, the Sisters gathered on the rocky shore, encircled by the arms of the half-beached leviathan.

Agnetta had been laid out on a flat bit of stone, out of reach of the sea, though the spray still drenched her. The wind battered the group, but in their thick diving suits, the Sisters wouldn't feel it. Quin, however, must be shivering, teeth chattering with the wet and the cold where they'd left him to kneel in the sand, hands bound.

Scribe IV had expected the Sisters to take Quin to the labyrinth. To the Chalice. He'd expected to have more time. But this hasty trial-and-execution all in one made him even more certain that the Sisters hadn't merely overlooked the clues and information he, Angel and Quin had uncovered. They had no interest in discovering the truth. They had come to the Bastion for purposes of their own.

His processors felt sludged, sand-clogged, salt-rotted. He couldn't see beyond this moment, couldn't think what to do. He felt not only cowardly, but powerless.

The Sisters had chosen a spot where the waters churned into a shallow bowl of eroded rock, a chalice formed by nature, much larger than the one in the labyrinth. They could Drown Quin right here.

The water glowed a green similar to the sky, but brighter, shadows visible within – fish spinning just below the surface to form a whirlpool at the Sisters' bidding. The Sisters' chanting was just audible over the waves – eerie, watery somehow, even on dry land. Changed as their jaws were, as their throats were, as their lungs were, rebuilt for life underwater.

"What do we do?" he repeated, losing track of how many times he'd asked, turning to look at Angel.

Since their retreat, Angel had shrunk xemself even smaller. Xe'd manifested wings, which arced over xyr body now, swallowing it in a protective cocoon. Xyr knees were drawn up against xyr chest, arms wrapped around xyr legs, face buried against them.

At Scribe IV's question, xe looked up. "There's something I can do," Angel said, the words barely a whisper.

Individual salt crystals shone in Angel's wind-wracked hair, no longer crackling with flames. Xyr face was salt-tracked as well, and Scribe IV doubted it was from the spray. Xe looked more like a child than ever. "I was afraid,"

Angel said. It sounded like the second half of the apology xe'd offered in the cave. "I'm still afraid now."

"Oh." It hadn't occurred to Scribe IV that an angel could feel fear.

Scribe IV could no longer sense the voice, that deep, shivering sound speaking words he couldn't hear. He wondered if Angel still could.

He crouched, joints whining in protest, and put a hand on Angel's shoulder. For once, Angel's eyes weren't smoke or fire, liquid gold or honey. They were green-gray, reflecting the sky, reflecting the sea.

Why had he assumed xe would be impervious to fear, to desire, to pain? Angel's behavior should have told him that if anything, xe felt everything more keenly, more fully. Perhaps every angel did. Every moment and any moment, they might burn in the pure fire of joy, or drown in the absoluteness of sorrow.

"I thought because they didn't pray, you couldn't..." Scribe IV let the words trail, afraid they sounded too much like blame.

Angel's eyes brimmed with unshed tears.

"The rules governing angels, like all rules, can be broken. But when they are..." Xe paused, taking a hitching breath. "The rules are there, and I follow them, because a worse thing will happen if I don't. If I do this, if I help Quin, I will change. I'm not sure how much, and once I do, I'm not sure I can change back again."

"I'm sorry." Scribe IV couldn't think of anything else to say. "Is there anything I can do?"

Angel shook xyr head. The motion rippled across xyr

body to become a pushing out of xyr chest, a squaring of xyr shoulders and wings. Xe didn't expand, but that only made it more impressive – xyr fragility against the weight of whatever it was xe intended to do. Angel stood, jutting out xyr chin. Xe moved to the mouth of the alcove above the sea, glancing back at Scribe IV, painful vulnerability etched clear in xyr narrow and pointed features, determination sealed over it.

"Stay with me." Angel's voice was very small. "Don't leave me, please, no matter what you see."

Before Scribe IV could question xem, Angel snapped xyr wings wide, a sound like thunder that buffeted him backward a step. Angel shot into the air, burning into the sky like a shooting star in reverse, a point of brightness against the sullen gray-green. Scribe IV imagined Angel as concentrated light, pulling into xemself, tumbling end over end in xyr upward fall until he lost sight of xem against the roiling clouds. Until he couldn't tell if xe had exploded into vastness to fill the sky, or if xe had simply reversed course in the smallness of xyr body and fallen.

The Sisters' chanting reached a fever pitch, and Scribe IV snapped his attention back to the rocky shore below. Whatever Angel was doing, would do, it seemed it would be too late. The leviathan hauled Quin into the air. The Sisters intoned their final words. The limb holding Quin aloft uncurled and let him fall into the whirling maw of the chalice below.

～

And in the chalice of whirling green, Aquinas St. John Drowned. As he Drowned, he saw – a slumbering god, far below the waves. His death, the first of many the Sisters had planned, not merely a death, but a prayer. A holy act not to wake their god, but to reshape them entirely, to make them a thing of the Sisters' will, not the other way around. Quin's terror, his pain, was once more the key to making a god. Even as he Drowned, inside all that terrible green, Quin screamed.

And far above the Bastion and the sea, in the void that was everywhere and nowhere, occupying every point in space and time, the angel Murmuration howled, a keening wail to shake the very foundation of Heaven.

And in the cave above the sea, time slowed to a syrupy crawl. Scribe IV braced himself and leaned outward.

Far below, Quin Drowned.

The wind battered Scribe IV, pushing him backward, tucking him away so he wouldn't have to see. Then, all at once, it dropped out. The waves calmed impossibly. The sea became flat glass, stealing the distinction between it and the sky.

The Sisters' chant faltered. The whirlpool froze. Was Quin still Drowning? Or had time truly stopped?

A vast shape, terrible in aspect and height, towered over the Sisters, at once as distant as the horizon and rising up from the water right against the shore. Angel. Scribe IV understood it to be xem, and not xem at the same time. Xe spoke, a voice that was many voices overlapping, as awful as xyr appearance had become.

"I am an angel of no mercy and I speak with the voice of God. Every god. Sisters of the Drowned, I speak to you now with the voice of *your* god."

Even up in the alcove, Scribe IV felt Angel's attention fall upon the Sisters – a weight, a shroud. It was the kind of attention that flayed, looked through skin, through bone, to the very core. The kind of attention that could take a person apart until they were nothing. No matter what they believed, or professed to believe.

"Too long, you have willfully misinterpreted Our dreams, claiming to act in Our name. All the while, you seek to remake Us in your image. If this angel, Our humble servant, but speaks a Holy Word, We will wake fully, and there will be nowhere in the seas below, or the Bastion above, or even among the stars, where you can hide."

Reality overlapped in planes, each as thin as a hair, as a breath, and as vast as all existence. Scribe IV saw Angel as he had known xem – like marble and like flame and like a child curled in the shadow of xyr wings. And he saw xem as a storm, covering the ocean, covering the Bastion, ready to wash this entire world clean. He saw xem as the Drowned God, not only speaking with their voice, but becoming them – ribs pressed outward against fish-eaten skin slit with gills, eyes churning with the tide, hair in ropes of kelp and seaweed, drowned and ever-drowning, dead and deathless, asleep and dreaming.

And in the vast depths, the same Drowned God whose voice tolled from Angel's lips turned over in their sleep. Scribe IV felt the very core of the planet shift. Felt the waters heave. He recognized the voice Angel spoke in, had felt it slither across his skin in the cavern above. He'd felt it calling to Angel, and xe'd finally answered, drawing it up from the depths of the sea to the cusp of waking, and holding it there. The shuddering attention that Angel had turned on the Sisters, but ten times over, a thousand times more terrible, was poised to break like a wave. And all that held it back in this moment was Angel.

Scribe IV wanted to duck, to wrap his arms around his head, crouch low and disappear. But he heard Angel's voice too, the moment before xe had taken to the sky.

Don't leave me.

Angel had been asking for more than Scribe IV's presence. Xe'd been asking Scribe IV not to be afraid. To see and know xem as an angel in all xyr awful glory, and not to turn away. Angel needed Scribe IV to witness xem, and still be xyr friend when all was said and done. To be an anchor to follow back to shore. The way Angel had been an anchor for Scribe IV, touching his shoulder, letting him know that he was not alone.

Scribe IV lowered his arms. He straightened his knees and lifted his head, forcing himself to keep looking at Angel, to keep looking at the Drowned God, and not turn away.

The Sisters, on the other hand, fled, scrambling, tripping over themselves and each other in their desperation to get back to the leviathan. Scribe IV recalled the way the

Mother Superior had blanched in Angel's presence. Now that xe spoke with the voice of her god, he imagined that all her blood had found a way to completely desert her body.

As the Sisters ran, their hold broke. The chalice coughed, giving Quin up. He landed roughly on the stones of the beach. The whirlpool dispersed, along with the glow and shadows of fish within it.

"Go now." Angel's voice rolled like a storm, making the leviathan shudder as its maw creaked shut and it struggled to haul itself back into the waves. "Pray and ask forgiveness, and learn again what it means to be a Sister of the Drowned."

The tide sloshed and lurched. The leviathan groaned, as if its rivets might pop, its bones might crack, but it slid back into the sea – a thing chastened and whipped. In its wake, Agnetta lay like an offering on the stone.

On the empty beach, Quin rolled onto his side, his body shuddering. The sea had released him, but Quin still Drowned. Quin would always be Drowning. That was the nature of the Sisters' punishment. Once enacted, the Drowning would never stop.

Angel folded back into xemself, landing on xyr knees next to Quin. Xe lifted him, even as his body fought and gasped and jerked in xyr arms. In a breath, xe appeared beside Scribe IV, xyr eyes large and filled with tears.

"We have to go now," Angel said. "We have to help him."

16

Lena had had her fill of angels. She certainly hadn't been expecting one to show up on her doorstep with an automaton in tow, holding her brother in its arms, all three of them soaking wet.

"What..." Lena kept her hand on the door, trying to make sense of the picture in front of her.

"We were on the beach," the angel said, as if that explained anything, as if the water beading on the automaton's gleaming skin, dripping from the cuffs of the angel's over-long sleeves, and soaking Quin's clothing, was the problem.

"What?" Lena repeated the question, more softly this time, stepping back to let them inside.

The angel's eyes were large in xyr narrow face, violet, frightened. Xe clutched Quin against xyr chest, looking like a child caught doing something wrong, gaze darting everywhere but somehow avoiding Lena's. It was the exact opposite of Starling's usual smug air. Lena did not want to think about how different his expression had been last time she'd seen him. So she focused on this angel instead, who looked like xe might cry at any moment.

"I'm very sorry, Ms. St. John." The automaton dipped his head slightly, respect and apology rolled into one. There was something almost musical in his voice, low and sonorous, doleful.

"I go by Vasquez, not St. John." She said the words by rote, unable to look away from her brother, limp in the angel's arms.

This must be Scribe IV and Angel, the ones Quin had told her about. But she still couldn't fathom their presence here, or what had happened.

Quin's head lolled back, his entire body shuddering. His skin looked like wax, his breathing fast and shallow.

"Ms. Vasquez, I'm sorry. Your brother Drowned." She heard the capital letter in Scribe IV's voice; the significance escaped her, but it still left her cold.

"Put him on the couch." Lena followed as Angel moved to obey.

She wanted to brush the damp hair from Quin's forehead. Before she could touch him, his eyes flew open – a strange sea-green they hadn't been before. His body snapped rigid, arching away from the couch like he was trying to escape himself, flesh pulling away from bone. He gasped, a wet and awful sound, and Lena stepped back, bumping into the angel, who caught and steadied her.

"Drown," Quin said. It sounded like his throat was full of rocks, gargling and painful to hear. "Sisters." He clawed at his throat, trying to spit the words out, still thrashing on her couch. "Drown the Bastion, remake their god."

Quin sank back on the couch, exhausted, shivering, still fighting. His eyes weren't focused. Lena could tell he didn't see her when she leaned over him, whispered his name.

"We may have gotten to him in time, but…" Angel began, and Lena whipped around to glare. Xe shrunk back from her, tucking xyr hands into xyr sleeves. Tears hovered in xyr eyes, making them look even larger.

"Who are you? What is he talking about? Who tried to remake a god?" Lena knelt next to Quin, touched his brow. He didn't react.

Remake their god. The words rang in her head, almost as terrible as the sight of her brother Drowning. Starling had only just eaten the memory of what their father had done from Quin's mind. If he'd witnessed someone else trying to make a god in their image, if he'd had to go through that all over again…

"I believe the Drowned Sisters sought to wake their god, but as a changed god, serving the purposes of their order, rather than the other way around. Your brother must have seen as much when they Drowned him."

The smell of brine clung to Quin. The only small mercy was that his body no longer arched and twisted. He rolled onto his side, arms wrapped around himself, jaw clenched hard and shuddering all over as if he were freezing.

"Lennie." Quin's eyes focused, and it was somehow worse. He unwrapped one arm from around his body and his fingers circled her wrist. His voice sounded as if he'd already spent ages at the bottom of the ocean, vocal cords salt-eaten, worn away. As if he were already dead. "I can't." The words broke into terrible stuttering gasps as Quin choked, as he fought to stay lucid and even so continued to Drown. "I can't. Please. You have to."

His grip tightened. Lena's eyes stung, nothing to do with the pain of Quin's cold fingers crushing her bones.

"Fuck." Lena knew what he was asking. She wished she didn't.

Quin let out another ragged gasp, a painful sound.

"Please." His eyes fluttered, fighting, fighting to stay with her.

He let go, body spasming again. She hauled in a wet breath, her own kind of choking. *Starling.* If she didn't take Quin to his angel and beg for his help, beg him to eat her brother's pain, then he would always be like this, perpetually Drowning. And this new pain, fear and desperate love, when all else was stripped away, might birth another god.

"You're a fucking angel. Can't you do something?" Lena rounded on Angel, who moved back a step as she rose from her crouch. She knew it wasn't fair. These were Quin's friends, they'd tried to help him, but her anger needed somewhere to go. "Can't you…?" She gestured, shoulders slumping. "Can't you get inside his head and fix it?"

Would it be any better to let this angel rummage around inside Quin?

Better the devil you know…

Angel's eyes widened. Xe held up xyr hands. "I promised your brother I wouldn't."

This startled Lena. She looked at Angel more closely. The fear hadn't left xyr eyes, and behind it, she saw something like sorrow. Xe bowed xyr head, speaking softly.

"The Drowned God is just under my skin. I'm afraid I would only hurt your brother if I tried." Xyr shoulders hunched inward.

She tried to imagine Starling looking like that. Tried to imagine a shiver like the one working its way across Angel's body now shaking him.

But she almost had seen that, hadn't she? The way Starling had spoken about Quin, the look in his eyes – she could almost believe the angel loved him.

"Then I need you to take him to someone who can help," Lena said. "He goes by the name of Starling. Sometimes Legion." She hesitated, exhaustion weighing her down all at once. "And sometimes Murmuration."

Was it her imagination, or did recognition flicker in the angel's eyes? Quin certainly reacted, a motion that somehow looked at once like pain and like longing, aching toward and away from the mere mention of his angel's name.

"Take your brother's hand," Angel said.

Lena grasped Quin's fingers, laced them with her own and held tight. His hand hung in hers, giving no sign he felt her presence. A memory assaulted her – Quin pulling her out of the dark. Out of the choking smell of death. He'd told her not to look, but she knew he had.

Lena closed her eyes. Everything shifted sideways. When she opened her eyes again, the white void greeted her. Quin's hand was still in hers, but Scribe IV and Angel were gone. Starling was there though, a jagged slash of ink against the whiteness. Quin floated upon it, splayed boneless and shivering.

"You have to help him, please," Lena said.

The angel's eyes were fathomless. For a moment, she imagined she could see her image reflected there, the tiniest mote in the vastness of his gaze.

"Always." Starling moved without seeming to move, his shoulder nudging Lena out of her place at Quin's side.

Her fingers pulled from her brother's. The angel replaced them with his own.

"Murmuration." Her brother's voice was faint as a whisper, but Lena saw his eyes focus on the angel, locking on him in a way that made her feel completely unnecessary.

Starling leaned over Quin, his expression one of awful tenderness and hunger. Lena's stomach twisted. She tried to blame the way the other angel had flung her through the vastness of space to get them here, which was nowhere, in the blink of an eye.

"You can't stay." Starling's voice was flat, and left no room for argument. "Wait in Quin's room."

He lifted his head, his gaze pinning her. The angel didn't push her physically, but Lena felt it nonetheless – a hand in the center of her chest, shoving her away. A last glimpse, as if from the far end of a long tunnel, of Starling leaning down, his lips at Quin's ear, and then she was in Quin's room, looking at his narrow bed. She just barely made it to the sink before vomiting.

The crack of wings, like a thousand birds taking flight at once, woke her. Lena didn't remember lying down. She ached with the aftermath of tears, a hollow feeling like a hangover. She sat up in the half-dark. At some point, the lights in Quin's room had dimmed of their own accord.

Starling caught himself with one long-fingered hand on the back of Quin's chair and stood there for a long time with his head bowed, hair hanging over his face. He shuddered, not quite crying, not quite the shivers that had wracked Quin's body. But there was an unevenness to his breath.

Lena remained still. She couldn't picture herself laying a hand on the angel's shoulder, forgiving him, comforting him, thanking him for what he'd done. The idea of touching him filled her with revulsion. It was so much easier to hate him, to want to hate him, than face the alternative – the idea of perfect, terrible love.

Starling raised his head, looked through her more than at her. "It's done."

Even in the dark, she could see the black of his eyes swirling with the thick, sluggish tide he'd taken from Quin. An unnatural green which made her seasick just looking at it. Lena forced herself up. Her legs felt numb. She had to look up to meet Starling's eyes. He seemed to have grown taller, more attenuated – as if in his pain, he'd forgotten how to appear human.

The gaze that met hers was hard-edged, like hatred, like blame. Instead of an image of herself floating there, she saw Starling himself, small and lost in the void. Lena's breath caught.

How dare she make him do this? How dare she ask for this, knowing he wouldn't refuse. What met her there was heartbreak. And she understood what Starling had done, what it had cost him.

"You ate away his memory of you, as well." It wasn't a question, and so Starling – Murmuration, she owed him that much at least – didn't dignify it with an answer. He turned his face away. Lena had the impression of his body as something like molten glass, stretched, twisted. In an instant it might harden and snap, but some strange force of will held it in this state, in-between.

"He's sleeping now. When he wakes, he won't remember where he was, but he'll know enough to come find you." There was resentment in his voice, and Lena understood – it was easier for the angel to hate her, to blame her, the way she'd wanted to hate and blame him.

Part of her wanted to ask why, but she was fairly certain she knew. Quin was an addict, always holding onto a little seed of his pain, letting it regrow, returning to the angel again and again to punish himself, to be forgiven. Murmuration was doing the only thing he could, walking away. But he would go on hurting, go on carrying Quin's pain alone.

An angel sorrowing was a terrible thing to behold.

"As I told you before, some wounds run too deep to heal. A wound caused by a god can only scar, never fully close." Starling showed teeth, a feral, gleeful, spiteful thing. For the space of a heartbeat, Lena thought the angel was gloating, reveling in the idea of what would happen the next time Quin's memories came for him. "You should have taken me up on my offer while you had the chance."

Then he was gone. Lena was left alone in Quin's room. The gravity of the station seemed to shift, tilting to compensate for the place where Murmuration no longer stood.

Her breath hitched. Lena was aware of tears on her cheeks, but she couldn't explain them. Not to herself, nor to Quin when the door slid open and he found her standing there in the dark, unable to do anything in the face of his quizzical expression except fold herself against him as she had once a very long time ago, arms around him, face buried against his neck, sobbing.

17

In the space between everything, Angel shuddered. Xe'd delivered Quin to the angel Murmuration as Lena had asked. Had xe done the right thing? Quin had been suffering, in pain. If xe'd acted sooner, if xe hadn't been afraid, could xe have stopped the Sisters before Quin Drowned?

It was xyr fault.

But the angel. The angel...

Xe'd never known one of xyr own kind so full of jagged edges. So full of hurt. Xe'd only brushed up against him briefly, accidentally, and it had been like scraping the rawest and most vulnerable parts of xemself against shattered glass.

Mouths. Murmuration looked like something human, if uncanny in his appearance, but beneath his skin, all Angel had seen was mouths, razor teeth, endless hunger.

Xe'd seen the broken places, too. The edges where the angel no longer fit together as a whole, where he'd been changed.

Angel had also changed. Even now, xe felt the subtle tug of divinity, like splinters left beneath xyr skin. Translucent fish swam between xyr ribs, nibbled at xyr flesh – even when xe did not have flesh. It would be too easy to break along the seams the Drowned God had left behind.

What if xe couldn't stop changing?

What if xe couldn't help but fall?

What if xe became a hungry thing like Murmuration, all jagged edges and mouths?

If Lena had not simply asked, but prayed; if Quin had asked himself, could Angel have eaten his memories? Would xe have been compelled? Even before that, in the cave, xe could have acted without compulsion, without prayer, if xe hadn't been so afraid. Xyr fear had earned them nothing: Quin had suffered, and the Drowned God had made a home in Angel's bones all the same.

If xe'd chosen to fall on xyr own terms, would it have been better?

Angel wondered – once upon a time, had Murmuration seen Quin's hurt and sought to soothe it? Or had Quin prayed, leaving Murmuration no choice but to answer? Xe'd heard Murmuration mourn in the moment Quin started to Drown. Xe'd felt it spread all across the firmament, shaking the very foundation of Heaven.

An angel could be a terrible thing, but so could a human, sometimes without even trying.

Hunger could cause an angel to fall, but so could love, and that was possibly the more terrible of the two.

If xe fell, would it be for hunger, or love?

Angel curled closer upon xemself, listening to the stars chime, trying to let their light bathe and soothe xem. But building somewhere in xyr core, xe felt a scream.

Xe let the light pull xem apart, becoming sound, becoming the ringing of bells, the chiming of gongs, the sound of fire upon the deep.

Angel gasped, a ragged noise without lungs, and the shuddering went on and on through xyr body, curling close, curling closer, a black hole collapsing inward, a dense star gathering mass before exploding to birth something new.

In the heart of that star, xe forgot to be anything but fear. In the next shuddering breath, xe recalled that Scribe IV had stayed with xem. When xe'd shrunk back into xemself after being a god, Scribe IV hadn't looked on xem with disgust or fear.

Love could save an angel, too.

Xe'd never been anything but Angel before, utterly xemself, with no need for any other name. Now xe'd changed, but that didn't mean Angel couldn't remain xemself. The offer xe'd made to Scribe IV held for Angel as well. Xe could choose what xe wanted to be.

The chiming bells stilled, the echoing gongs fading so only the soft melody of the stars remained. Light bathed xem. Angel slowly drifted back into xemself, pulled inward, gathering the pieces of xyr being into something new – a shape like a prayer, smelling of warm wax and honey. Not a school of fish, but a hive, the hum of wings reminding xem that xe was not alone – not if xe didn't want to be.

Scribe IV was only ever a breath away. He had saved Angel, even if he didn't realize it. Scribe IV was xyr friend.

The last fragments of Angel settled together, the tension and fear unwinding from xem. Xe would return to the Bastion, to Scribe IV, and find a way to thank him.

18

"I never thought I'd see this day. Honestly, I'm worried you brought me here to tell me I'm dying or something." Quin looked between Rowan and his sister.

He said it lightly, but the glance that passed between them, the one they didn't quite manage to hide, created a lump in his throat. Rowan and Lena, sharing some kind of secret he couldn't fathom. It made him itchy. He wanted to reach inside and pull the irritant from under his skin.

"Not dying, honey, but you did give us quite a scare." Rowan covered Quin's hand with his own, each finger weighted by a ring with a gem almost as big as an eyeball, flashing in the light.

Quin had been sick. Some weird bug he'd picked up in the Bastion while investigating a case. The fever had laid him low for days, which he thankfully didn't remember. It was unsettling, though, having only Lena and Rowan's account of his illness, how they had taken turns looking after him.

It wasn't just the illness, either – even the days preceding it felt blurry, gaps in his thoughts and recollections. Things he should know, but didn't.

He'd solved the case he'd been working on, the credits in his account told him that much. Part of him wished he could remember more, but any time he probed the memory, it was like touching a wound that hadn't fully healed. Maybe some things were better left untouched.

A waiter circled past, depositing a second pitcher of mimosas. He'd never been to Cirque during the day, but Rowan promised they did a killer brunch. The plates scattered between them were evidence that he'd been right.

"Seriously, though, since when did you two get chummy?" Quin lifted his glass, held it without sipping, and looked between Lena and Rowan again.

He should let it go, but he'd never been capable of doing that. He had to peer into the dark corners, look under the rocks, pick at the scab even though he knew it would leave a scar. If he kept pushing, eventually one of them would crack. His bet was on Rowan.

He just wanted one of them to explain the tense silence, why they kept looking at him like any minute, he might shatter.

"We're family," Lena said, but her gaze slid away, and the words seemed to stick in her throat. "I want us to spend more time together. I figure that includes getting to know your friends and perhaps accepting that I may have judged them too harshly in the past."

"Why, Ms. Vasquez, did you just come close to saying

a nice thing about me?" Rowan put a hand to his chest, affecting shock, batting his eyes.

Even off stage, he was dressed with impeccable, glorious style. No wings or shimmering gown, but his lilac wig and makeup were utter perfection. His flowy blouse and loose, wide-legged pant combo shifted with the iridescence of a soap bubble. He'd at least opted for sensible, flat open-toed sandals instead of platforms or stilettoes, but brunch – as he'd told Quin – was still an Occasion with a capital O, for which one dressed seriously and with intention.

"Don't get cocky." Lena raised an eyebrow and sipped from her drink.

Rowan snorted, a most unladylike sound. Quin couldn't help a chuckle.

"I'll take it, for now, but don't think I'm going to let my guard down. I still half-suspect you're planning to team up to steal my kidney and sell it on the black market or something," Quin said.

"Honey, no one wants your busted-ass old kidneys. Now be a good boy, drink up, and stop worrying."

Rowan refilled Quin's glass while Lena snagged a last piece of cooling bacon from one of the plates.

Don't pick it, or it'll bleed. It'll scar.

The voice in his head was eminently sensible. There was something – maybe the lingering effects of the fever leaving his system – that made him feel like he was balanced on a tightrope, suspended over a very long fall. Ahead of him was a wide-open vista. If he kept his head up and made himself walk across, a myriad of possibilities awaited him. He could go anywhere, do anything. But if he looked down, looked back, the only possibility would be to fall.

His best friend and his sister watched him expectantly, trying to pretend they weren't doing exactly that.

"To fresh starts, and letting go, I suppose." Quin tapped his glass against his sister's and Rowan's in turn.

Even over the susurrus filling the bar, the sound of glass on glass rang in Quin's ears. Not the chime it should be – for no reason at all that he could explain, it reminded him of birds taking flight, the stuttering clap of a thousand wings.

19

A change in air pressure heralded Angel's return. Scribe IV hadn't seen xem since xe'd taken Quin to be healed. Three weeks, two days, seven hours and forty-six minutes precisely. But for all the precision built into him, the images Scribe IV held in his head as he turned to look at his guest were contradictory – Angel as a child, dripping hair plastered to xyr skin and long sleeves covering xyr nervous fingers; Angel vast as the sky over the Bastion, speaking with the voice of a god; Angel burning and burning, flames crackling in xyr hair.

This time, Angel brought with xem the scent of beeswax; Scribe IV could smell it, although such a thing should be impossible. It was like a candle burning somewhere and producing a comforting golden light. Xe'd forgotten or chosen not to be human for the moment. Half xyr face was honeycomb, humming with wings. Xyr chest was open, ribs dripping with honey, a hive in place of xyr heart.

But as Scribe IV rose from his desk, Angel smiled, folding back down into something like a taller, less frightened version of the child Scribe IV had last seen. Xe still smelled of beeswax, and the ghost of what xe'd been, what xe'd become to save Quin from the Sisters, lingered behind xyr eyes.

"Are you alright?" Scribe IV asked.

The question seemed to startle Angel, xyr eyes widening.

Gratitude, at least that's what Scribe IV thought it was. All at once, Angel threw xyr arms around him, a hug that nearly knocked him over, despite the slightness of xyr frame. When xe stepped back, grinning, it almost looked like xe was blushing.

"I wasn't certain you'd return." Scribe IV poured a measure from the heavy glass decanter – a comforting bit of hospitality that felt like safer ground than probing the angel's sudden display of emotion, or sorting out how that emotion made Scribe IV himself feel.

Angel held the glass without bringing it to xyr lips. Behind the troubled expression in xyr eyes lay curiosity. Scribe IV felt studied, a puzzle for Angel to figure out. Could xe see the aches in his joints, the faint patina to his skin? Or had he only imagined all those things – an automaton dreaming of age, dreaming of the kind of death that could never exactly come for him?

"I wasn't certain you would stay," Angel countered, finally sipping xyr drink, letting only the faintest glimmer of flame swirl in its depths.

"Neither was I." Scribe IV had considered leaving, but where else was there to go?

The past three weeks had been an endless barrage of people flowing through the Bastion, more perhaps than would even have attended the conclave. It had been relentless. Authorities from all sectors were trying to untangle the knot of Agnetta and her brother's crime. Delegations from every religion, sect and branch, half-forgotten groups and orders whose names Scribe IV hadn't heard spoken in years. Not just humans either, but bodhisattvas and saints, angels and demons, things that had been human, long ago, and things that never had. Scribe IV had even glimpsed the godling who had once been a child hiding in the caverns beneath the Bastion.

In all that time, he hadn't seen Angel, or Quin, or even Lena.

Having no kin aside from the half-brother she'd helped to murder, and the twin who'd helped her do the deed, Agnetta had been laid to rest in the garden outside the Bastion's walls. Her brother had been apprehended fleeing Ganymede.

Scribe IV had re-integrated the memory of the night twenty-two years ago – Agnetta, a swaddled baby, carried inside the Bastion, her mother and brother disappearing into the storm – into his primary core. The empty capsule that had once held the memory hung from a chain he now wore about his neck. He wouldn't forget again; he owed them that much – more, but it was all he could do.

The question of who would become the next pope troubled him. The possibility of the Drowned Sisters' return troubled him more. They'd swooped in like opportunistic fish feeding off whale fall, using the Pope's death as a means to carry out their own plans. Scribe IV had known they'd strayed from their god's will, but he hadn't realized how far.

They would have Drowned the whole Bastion to remake their god in their own image – horror as devotion, like the Drownings of old, but on a massive scale.

Would it have been enough? And without Angel there to stop them, would the Sisters try again?

"Will you stay?" Angel asked, pulling Scribe IV from his grim thoughts.

"I'm not sure where else I would go."

If the Sisters did return, there was little he could do to stop them. So why stay? The Pope's murder felt like punctation at the end of a sentence and an era. The Bastion was already half-forgotten. Scribe IV could easily see how it would only slide further into decline. What had happened here would echo, a haunting that would turn people away. Pilgrims would forget this had once been a holy site. Even the prayers might dry up eventually; a Scribe with nothing to record. He could simply let entropy take its toll.

"You could go anywhere, be anything you choose." Angel spoke to the thoughts he hadn't voiced.

Scribe IV supposed he could, indeed, be anything. Angel had the power to gift him as much. An extraordinary miracle, undoing him at the very base level of his existence and weaving him into something new.

Choice. A momentous thing. He had never been offered one before. It was wondrous, and terrifying. He'd spent so long feeling the weight of his age; now all at once, Scribe IV felt unprepared. He needed more time.

"Is there…?" He fumbled the words, which an automaton was not meant to do. He tried again. "Can I choose later, if I remain here a while?"

"Of course." Angel smiled. It was soft, like a glimmer of candlelight, like melting beeswax. Melancholy still shadowed xem – a scar that would perhaps never heal – but it seemed to Scribe IV xe was learning to live with it, or would learn to live with it, in time.

Scribe IV wanted to believe that his own purpose would become clear in time as well. Faith in a world where gods were proven – maybe that in itself was a mystery worth investigating. The riddle of himself, his purpose in life, and what he might become.

"Until I figure it out, I will remain, then." Scribe IV paused, feeling almost shy voicing the next part out loud. "Will you still come visit sometimes?"

"Of course," Angel said again, and this time xyr smile lit xyr face, unshadowed and genuine.

Scribe IV deeply wished he could return Angel's smile. He inclined his head instead, hoping xe understood.

"Until then," Scribe IV said.

Angel's smile became a flash, brilliant as a star being born, swallowing xem whole. When the light faded, Angel was gone, leaving Scribe IV alone in the room. Even so, Angel's voice echoed. Scribe IV heard xyr words clear as a ringing bell.

"I'm only ever as far away as a prayer."

Scribe IV had only ever recorded prayers for others. With Angel listening, he looked forward to offering up one of his own.

He tilted his head back to watch the rolling green sky and the slow progression of three rising moons.

ACKNOWLEDGEMENTS

This book started, as so many of the things I've written do, as a stray thought, a handful of images, a few lines. A whole slew of wonderful people helped me along the way, shaping *Out of the Drowning Deep* into the book you hold in your hands, and I am so very grateful to all of them.

A conversation with Scott Andrews, walking back from dinner at some convention or other, started this whole thing snowballing in my mind. E. Catherine Tobler and Eugenia Triantafyllou were wonderful and generous first readers, helping me reflect and refine when I desperately thrust a handful of virtual pages their way and asked them, "Is this anything?"

My agent, Barry Goldblatt, helped me further hone my vision, and found the novella a good home. Katie Dent brought a keen editorial eye, and through several patient revisions helped cut away what wasn't needed and add what should have been there all along. The entire team at Titan made sure the book looks wonderful, and Nat MacKenzie gave it an absolutely stunning cover.

Fran and Tom Wilde hosted a wonderful writing retreat weekend, which was just what I needed to get vital revisions done. A. T. Greenblatt, Stephanie Feldman, Siobhan Carroll, Fran Wilde, and Sarah Pinsker collectively remain the most incredible group of writing/critique buddies and friends a person could ask for, and they are a constant source of encouragement and inspiration.

Derrick, Amy, and Matt, you are my people. Thank you for being ridiculous with me, for always being there, and for just being you.

My family, near and far, blood and otherwise, you are amazing, and I wouldn't be where I am today without you.

To the writing community in general, folks I've chatted with online and at conventions, hung out with, shared meals with, been on panels with, and even those I haven't met yet – thank you for all that you do. Keep making beautiful art and telling the stories only you can tell.

And last, but not least, thank you to Pippin, Pond, and Luna. You keep me company while writing, but you are very rarely helpful. You bark and shed, knock things over, and demand food at weird hours, but I love you, and I wouldn't have it any other way.

ABOUT THE AUTHOR

A. C. Wise is the author of *Wendy, Darling, Hooked,* and *Out of the Drowning Deep,* along with the short story collection, *The Ghost Sequences.* Her work has won the Sunburst Award for Excellence in Canadian Literature of the Fantastic, and has been a finalist for the Nebula, Bram Stoker, World Fantasy, Locus, British Fantasy, Aurora, Lambda Literary, and Ignyte Awards. In addition to her fiction, she contributes a review column to *Apex Magazine* and *Locus Magazine.*

WENDY, DARLING

by A. C. Wise

A lush, feminist re-imagining of what happened to Wendy after Neverland, for fans of *Circe* and *The Mere Wife*. Locus Award finalist for Best First Novel.

Find the second star from the right, and fly straight on 'til morning, all the way to Neverland, a children's paradise with no rules, no adults, only endless adventure and enchanted forests – all led by the charismatic boy who will never grow old.

But Wendy Darling grew up. She has a husband and a young daughter called Jane, a life in London. But one night, after all these years, Peter Pan returns. Wendy finds him outside her daughter's window, looking to claim a new mother for his Lost Boys. But instead of Wendy, he takes Jane.

Now a grown woman, a mother, a patient and a survivor, Wendy must follow Peter back to Neverland to rescue her daughter and finally face the darkness at the heart of the island…

"Intelligent and deftly executed." TOR.com

For more fantastic fiction, author events,
exclusive excerpts, competitions, limited editions and more

VISIT OUR WEBSITE
titanbooks.com

LIKE US ON FACEBOOK
facebook.com/titanbooks

FOLLOW US ON TWITTER AND INSTAGRAM
@TitanBooks

EMAIL US
readerfeedback@titanemail.com